As soon as she saw me, Raquel Gross clicked her switchblade phone closed as if there hadn't been anyone on the other end and hurried around her glass and steel desk to enfold me in a huge embrace.

"I am *so excited*," she said, rocking me back and forth.

"Me too," I tried to say, though she was holding me so tight it came out as "Mmm-tuh."

"You . . . are . . . going . . . to . . . be . . . a . . . star," she said, separating the words like that.

"Wow."

"I'm so glad you decided to sign," she said, bustling back to her side of the desk and motioning for me to sit. "That is *so* the right decision. I mean, 'Should I pursue a fabulous modeling career or do nothing in nowheresville?' Duh!"

When I didn't laugh, she cleared her throat and shuffled through the papers in front of her.

"All right," she said, pushing the first thick stack of papers toward me. "Initial here and here and here, and sign here, and, let me see, here."

I picked up the document, thick and dense as a history paper, except neater, and started reading.

"What are you doing?" Raquel said.

"I'm reading it."

She snapped her scarlet-tipped fingers in the air. "This is New York!" she cried. "People do things fast here! They don't read their contracts."

The Home for Wayward
SUPERMODELS

Pamela Satran

doWn
tOwn
press

NEW YORK LONDON TORONTO SYDNEY

Fiction

 Downtown Press
A Division of Simon & Schuster, Inc.
1230 Avenue of the Americas
New York, NY 10020

First Downtown Press trade paperback edition July 2007

DOWNTOWN PRESS and colophon are trademarks of
Simon & Schuster, Inc.

For information about special discounts for bulk purchases,
please contact Simon & Schuster Special Sales at 1-800-456-6798
or business@simonandschuster.com

Designed by Mary Austin Speaker
Illustrations by Sara Singh

Manufactured in the United States of America

10 9 8 7 6 5 4 3 2 1

ISBN-13: 978-1-4165-1691-0
ISBN-10:   1-4165-1691-3

For the Satran Family of Eagle River, with love

Acknowledgments

I was, through one of those amazing New York accidents, a fashion editor at *Glamour* for six years, which taught me all I know about the world of fashion shoots and supermodels.

A special thanks to my longtime partner in fashion crime, Kim Bonnell, for always making that world fun and challenging, and to Lisa Lebowitz Cader, Cindi Leive, Lauren Brody, and the late great Ruth Whitney for being wonderful and lasting connections to the *Glamour* experience. Thank you, too, to Judy Coyne, originator of the *Glamour List,* who launched me on the form.

My Eagle River, Wisconsin family, parents-in-law Dan and Betty Satran; sisters-in-law Jane, Jone, and Mitzi; brothers-in-law Dan, John, Tom, and Tim; outlaws Leslie, Mike, Chuck, Carol, Steve, and Holly; along with my husband, Dick, have over the years generously embraced me and made me feel part of their beautiful corner of the world. Special thanks to Mitzi for the insightful tour of the Rhinelander airport and to Tom for the outdoorsman's perspective.

On the publishing front, I owe eternal gratitude to my ever-wise and supportive agent Deborah Schneider, and to the formidable executives of Downtown Press—Louise Burke, Amy Pierpont, Lauren McKenna, and Megan McKeever—who expertly guided this book from conception to reality.

And a special thanks to my son, Owen, who convinced me to write it in the first place.

The Home for Wayward SUPERMODELS

one

Maybe I was holding on to Tom so tight at the airport because some part of me knew I wouldn't be coming back, at least not the way I planned, and not for a long time.

But that day, my clinginess just seemed strange. All I'd been thinking about for months and months was the trip to New York my mom was taking me on as a combination graduation/birthday/last-and-next-Christmas present, and then when we got to the airport I couldn't stop holding on to

Tom. Suddenly I didn't want to go, didn't want to leave him for even one minute, couldn't imagine why I ever wanted to see New York in the first place, even though I'd been dying to go there my entire life.

"Let's tell them now," I whispered to Tom.

My lips brushed the edge of his tattered green fishing cap, fragrant with the trout he'd caught that morning and a hundred other mornings before. Tom was the only boy in Eagle River who was both taller than me and liked my height, as well as most everything else about me. He'd delayed a trolling trip to Big Secret Lake with a high-paying client to be here at the Rhinelander, Wisconsin, airport with me.

I felt him shake not just his head, but his entire lean and muscular body, as resistant as a hooked rainbow. It wasn't like Tom to waste a word when he didn't have to, even as short a one as *no*. But he was adamant that we were not going to tell my parents that we'd decided to get married until after my eighteenth birthday, which I'd be celebrating in New York with Mom.

"I'm scared," I whispered.

I was afraid that going on this trip would be like the pebble that starts the avalanche, the one tiny change that would set off the reaction that would somehow transform everything. I loved things exactly like they were right now. Blinking back tears as I stared over Tom's broad shoulder at the Oneida casino posters, I thought maybe Tom would meet someone else while I was in New York, and that by the time I got back he wouldn't want to marry me anymore.

But Tom believed I meant I was scared of the flight, or of New York itself. He gathered me in close and hugged me with those arms that were stronger than he knew, so tight that all the tears popped right out of my eyes, blinding me. I had to think so hard about breathing then that I stopped feeling scared. I kept meaning to complain about the tightness of those hugs, except I was afraid that would make him stop giving them to me.

I heard my dad clear his throat and then Mom said, "It's time, Amanda."

Then Tom shocked me by giving me an enormous kiss, right on the lips, with tongue, in front of my parents and everyone. For once, it was me who pulled back, just in time to see my dad reel around and pretend to be deeply interested in the Avis sign.

"Amanda," said my mom, reaching out her dimpled arm to me.

"Please," I said to Tom, gripping his waist.

But instead of answering me he stripped off his fishing vest, the one decorated with all his favorite flies in the world, and handed it to me. Then, without a word, he turned around and headed toward the door and the parking lot beyond, waving over his head so I would know he was still thinking about me, even if he could not show me his face. He and Dad were driving home together, so Dad watched after him nervously, and then moved to kiss first me and then Mom on the cheek.

"Have fun, you two," he said. And then he too was gone.

As I moved zombielike with Mom through the makeshift security gate, where they actually made me take off my sock monkey slippers and send them through the X-ray machine, I tried to think of ways to distract myself from my near overwhelming feeling of dread. Here's what I did:

1. Took breaths so deep I swear I could feel them in the crotch of my cutoffs.

2. Tried to imagine what kind of underwear each of the other ten passengers waiting for our connecting flight to Milwaukee was wearing.

3. Imagined all the celebrities—from P. Diddy to the Olsen twins—I might get to meet in New York.

4. Held my mom's soft hand, damp because she was so nervous she'd been up since 4 a.m., packing and repacking her already packed suitcase.

5. Mentally walked myself through all the steps involved in making my mom's special deep-dish apple pie, the best-selling selection at Patty's House O' Pies. (Mom is Patty, and the pie store is off the main street of Eagle River right next to my dad's shop, Duke's House O' Bait. They tried combining them as Duke and Patty's House O' Pies 'N' Bait, thinking the delicious smell of Mom's pies might make Dad's shop smell better, but unfortunately the opposite happened.) Anyway, thinking about making the pie made me feel better until I remembered that the last deep-dish apple I made was for Tom, and then I wanted to break down again.

Finally it was time to file out onto the tarmac and into the tiny plane, where the flight attendant who gave us the safety lecture and the pilot were the same person. I gripped my armrests and closed my eyes until we were high in the sky and the plane leveled off. Then I finally let out my breath and peered from my window, trying to find Eagle River and any place in it that meant anything to me. I could not pick out our old red house or the shops but I did spot Big Secret Lake, and imagined Tom and me on the island where we always camped there, doing nothing but making lazy love and fishing for days on end. I felt at that moment that Tom was always with me, like the sky or the land, and that realization finally brought the comfort that imagining underwear and even holding my mom's hand did not.

When we landed in Milwaukee, I stood up and opened the overhead bin, intending to retrieve my suitcase. But it wasn't there. It was not under the seat in front of me either, and I definitely had not checked it at the airport. The last I remembered was setting down the suitcase—the suitcase filled with all the new clothes that Mom had bought me specially for this trip—right before I hugged Tom, right before I whispered those things in his ear. The suitcase was still in Rhinelander, it was clear, and now I would be making my grand entrance in New York wearing cutoff jeans, a House O' Pies T-shirt, Tom's fishing vest, and the sock monkey slippers on my feet.

· · ·

When Mom burst into tears as the Empire State Building came into view from the bus from LaGuardia Airport, I thought it was because she was upset about my leaving the suitcase behind.

"I'll use my own money to replace the clothes," I told her, thinking that instead of going to Wisconsin Dells for our honeymoon, as we'd hoped, Tom and I could just go on our usual weekend-after-Labor Day trip to the island in Big Secret. "My friend Desi promised me she'd show me all the cheap places to shop."

Contemplating buying an entirely new wardrobe with Desi made me feel as excited as the sight of all those tall buildings shining on the sunny horizon, like some non-Emerald but even-more-beautiful Oz. I'd met Desi online, in a vintage clothing lovers' chat room, way before I knew I'd ever get to go to New York. I'd sent her a House O' Pies shirt and a genuine coonskin cap from the St. Vincent DePaul shop; she sent me her mom's old flamenco shoes and a pink fur stole that would have looked swell on Gina Lollobrigida, one of my vintage style icons. Anticipating not only going shopping with Desi but *having* to buy clothes erased the final traces of feeling sad about missing Tom.

"I don't mind about the clothes," Mom said, sniffling. "I'm just so tickled to be here again."

I tore my eyes away from the skyline ahead. "Again?"

"I mean I'm tickled again," she said, attempting a smile. "As thrilled as I was on Christmas morning when you unwrapped your ticket."

"Me too, Mom."

As soon as we checked into the Holiday Inn on the edge of Chinatown, recommended by Desi because it was cheap, near all the coolest neighborhoods, *and* five minutes from her apartment, I dialed Desi's number. When she heard my voice, she let out a scream so loud it made my heart stop.

"Are you okay?" I asked her, alarmed.

"Oh my God, that's so cute the way you say that, *oo-key,*" she said. "Yes, I'm *oo-key!* I'm just so freaking excited! What's wrong with you? Aren't you excited?"

Of course I was excited, but in Eagle River, we screamed like that only if we were in the middle of being murdered, and even then, we'd try to tone it down. Don't want to make a big fuss, you know. Better not to draw attention to yourself.

I shot a glance at my mom, who was squeezing around the furniture crowded into the tiny room, putting away her clothes and humming "New York, New York."

"I'm excited," I assured Desi.

"You don't sound excited."

This was the first time, after emailing nearly every day for a year, we'd actually talked on the phone, and it was weird. The voice I'd heard in my head when I was reading her emails, which sounded like my own, did not match the voice that was coming through the phone, which sounded like Adriana's on *The Sopranos.*

"Can we meet right away?" I said, imagining my voice was a car engine and I was pressing the gas pedal to the floor. "I lost my suitcase and I need to go shopping because all I have to wear on my feet are sock monkey slippers and I think my mom's hungry."

Mom refolded a pair of her gigantic underpants, hot pink and wide as a pillowcase, and nodded vigorously. It was way past lunchtime, and all they'd given us on the plane was a stale roll and a wedge of plasticized cheese.

"Okay," said Desi decisively. "We'll meet in ten minutes at the Dancing Chicken."

"The Dancing Chicken?" Was that a nightclub? A fast-food place?

"Well, there's no chicken anymore. Cruelty to animals or something, so they probably killed it." Desi laughed. "But the sign still says Dancing. Dancing and Tic-Tac-Toe. It's the Chinatown Arcade, on Mott Street, just a few blocks from you. Anyone can tell you how to get there."

"Wait, wait!" I said, afraid Desi was about to hang up. "How will I know you?"

She laughed again, as dryly as she had when she said they killed the chicken.

"I'll be wearing a red flower bigger than my head."

· · ·

There was only one person wearing a big red flower at the Dancing Chicken, and it was someone much darker, shorter, and curvier than I believed Desi to be. Although we'd traded photos online, we'd turned it into a joke, always doing ourselves up in hats and wigs and makeup and masks, so that it was impossible to tell what we each really looked like. I approached, waiting for her to give me a sign.

But she looked right at me, even down at the monkeys on my feet, and then back toward the door.

"Hi," I said.

Again she looked at me, but just as quickly moved away, as if she thought I might try to snatch her purse.

"I guess that's not her," I told Mom.

Though the place was packed with people coming in and out, more people than there were in the hallway at Northland Pines High School after the final bell, no one else showed up wearing a red flower.

People showed up wearing a lot of other interesting things, however. In fact, this crowd made my fishing vest getup look positively normal. Watching everyone who came in and out, I decided there are Some Things You Can Tell About People from Their Clothes:

1. Where they stand on the comfort versus beauty issue.
2. How hot they want you to think they are. (But not how hot they really are. Witness my personal hottie, Tom, and his smelly cap.)
3. How much they need their clothes to help them look cool.
4. How much they want to fit in or stand out.
5. Whether they know how to use an iron.
6. Whether they know what's worth the money.
7. How much they care about what other people think.

And Some Things You Can't:

1. How much money they actually have. I'm talking about artfully bleached and torn jeans that cost three hundred dollars. I'm also talking about cubic zirconia.
2. Whether their souls match their clothes.

I saw a couple of people cast glances at Mom, who was dressed in one of her polyester print dresses, big enough for a whole family to camp in, and look away, stifling a snicker. Or not even stifling.

I hated those dresses too, but I hated the people making fun of them even more. One woman, wearing a sleeveless white linen dress I knew was Calvin Klein, looked at Mom and then clapped her hand over her mouth, like she was about to throw up. I wanted to grab her by the throat and tell her that inside my mom was the one dressed in an eleven-hundred-dollar white linen dress, and that she was the one in the psychic muumuu, but she was obviously not the kind of person who would comprehend that. Besides, that would embarrass Mom, who was standing there patiently waving her hand in front of her neck in an attempt to stay cool.

"Maybe I should just get a pretzel from that cart over there," Mom finally said.

But Mom had been trying so hard to do low-carb all spring, not even eating the crust on her own pies, her favorite part.

"I'm sure Desi'll be here in a minute."

We waited some more.

"Or a little container of those Chinese noodles," Mom said. "Do you think those have many calories?"

I looked at Mom. We'd been standing there for more than half an hour. "You shouldn't worry about calories; we're on vacation," I said, stretching my arm around her shoulder. "Maybe I should call Desi."

One of Mom's best customers, one of the rich summer people who were crazy for her pies, had lent her a cell phone just for this trip. Mom had promised that we would use it only in case of emergency, though the customer had insisted it didn't matter. "Just don't talk more than eight hundred minutes," the customer had said, laughing.

Mom took the phone out of her purse and handed it to me as carefully as if it were a pistol. I dialed. Desi answered immediately.

"Where are you?" she snapped—or more accurately, *Wheh aw you?*

I looked around, surprised. "I'm in the Dancing Chicken," I said. "Where are you?"

"*I'm* in the Dancing Chicken," said Desi, "and you're not here."

"Just a second," I said.

I stopped the first person walking by, an Asian man wearing a dirty apron and carrying a pink tray loaded with clean glasses.

"Excuse me, sir," I said. "Is this the Dancing Chicken?"

He nodded. "Yes. But no more chicken."

"Did you hear that?" I asked Desi. "We are definitely in the Dancing Chicken."

"Near the entrance?"

"Right next to the entrance, in front of the place with the parasols hanging out front."

There was a moment of silence, and then she said, "What do you look like?"

"I'm tall," I said. "Skinny. And like I told you, I have monkeys on my feet."

Now I noticed that the dark young woman wearing the red flower, the one I'd tried to talk to when we first came in, was standing directly across from me. Holding a cell phone to her ear. And looking straight into my eyes.

"You didn't tell me," she said.

It was her. The words coming out of the phone were the same ones I could read on her lips.

"Didn't tell you what?"

"You didn't tell me that you were freaking gorgeous."

I was so dumbstruck that I was still working my mouth, trying to come up with a response, when she flipped her phone closed and strode over to me, right up close, so she had to crane her head back to look up at me, and I had to peer down to where she stood with her chin jutting into my chest.

"But I'm not gorgeous," I stammered. "The kids call me giraffe. I drink a milkshake every day and my bones still stick out. My teeth are crooked. Tom is the only guy who has ever even *wanted* to kiss me."

Desi pursed her lips and looked at Mom. "She's gorgeous," Desi said. *Gawjus.* "Am I right?"

Mom nodded, surveying me. "I've been trying to tell her so for years."

I rolled my eyes. "You have to say that. You're my mom."

"She comes by it naturally," Mom explained to Desi, ignoring me. "I was a model myself, back in the eighties."

"Wow," said Desi. "So do you think Amanda could be a model too?"

"Mom was a model in *Milwaukee*," I interrupted, before they could get too carried away with this ridiculous conversation. "Come on, we're wasting valuable shopping time."

A smile began to spread across Desi's face. "So you're dying to hit the downtown thrift stores?"

"Can't wait!"

The main passion Desi and I had in common was clothes. She loved to design them, and I loved wearing them.

"You also want to see the fashion hot spots of SoHo and NoLita?" she asked.

"You know I do."

"But first you'd like to stop for maybe some shrimp lo mein or tagliatelle bolognese?"

"Mmmmmm," said Mom.

Which was my only clue that what Desi was talking about was food. And suddenly I was totally hungry. "Whatever you say."

"So what are we waiting for?" said Desi. "Let's go."

. . .

Here are some stores that did *not* whet our shopping appetites:

1. A Chinese butcher shop that sold ducks' feet and pigs'
   snouts.
2. A Chinese fish shop with eels hanging in the window like
   slimy black ribbons.
3. Prada. *Gawjus,* as Desi would say, but about a bazillion
   dollars out of our price range.
4. A gallery showing photographs of nude people in Third
   World countries who were missing limbs or eyes or were
   even more voluptuous than Desi or bonier than me. I
   couldn't stop staring at them in the gallery but couldn't
   imagine wanting to face one over my cereal every morning,
   even if they hadn't cost $8,000.
5. Hideously Ugly Hooker Shoes. That's not what it was
   really called, but should have been.
6. Smelly Clothes Last Worn By Dead People. See above.
7. Chanel. See Prada.
8. A tiny store presided over by an even tinier Japanese
   woman, where all the clothes were minuscule, far too short
   for me and way too narrow for Desi. They looked like chihuahua clothes. We laughed and laughed.

After the chihuahua-clothing store, Mom said she was really
exhausted and that Desi and I should go on without her. We
dropped her back at the hotel, figuring we had only an hour
left until the stores closed.

"We're going wild now," Desi informed me, as soon as we

were back on the street. "I'll take you to all my really favorite places."

Desi's legs may have been nearly a foot shorter than mine, but she managed to move a lot faster than me, weaving her way through the people and the dogs and the garbage like some kind of urban athlete. I had to trot to keep up, and kept tripping over things and bumping into people, spending a lot of time saying "Excuse me," which made people look at me as if I were totally loony. Which made *me* want to say "Excuse me" for saying "Excuse me."

Here are some stores we went to where we *did* buy something—and what we bought:

1. A tiny shop on Canal Street, where I bought a Rolex (Desi called it a Fauxlex) plus a fake Marc Jacobs bag for twenty dollars, total.
2. Pearl River Trading: flip-flops to walk in (good night, monkey slippers!), a sari, and a straw bag big enough to be my new suitcase.
3. Canal Jean: four XXL T-shirts—orange, turquoise, yellow, and magenta—Desi promised to recut into dresses for me.
4. A shoe repair shop piled with dusty shoes no one had ever picked up, where we found a rack of sunglasses from the seventies with bright blue and taxi yellow lenses that were a dollar each.
5. A clothing-and-music trading store, where I traded my House O' Pies T-shirt (don't worry: the fishing vest covered everything) for ten CDs.
6. A funky pharmacy: false eyelashes. Plus a toothbrush, shampoo, conditioner, and white lipstick.

7. An Italian coffee shop, where I ate my first cannoli. Which tasted so good I ate another one.

8. A shop called Frock that had the most amazing vintage clothes, everything from Comme des Garçons to Balenciaga and pre-Ford Gucci, where Desi went to get inspiration for her own designs.

I didn't actually buy anything there, but that's where it all started, or at least the New York part of it.

I'm talking about my modeling career, and it's ironic that the thing that launched it was my overindulgence in the cannolis.

What happened was that I took two dresses into the changing room. One was this very simple but extra-clingy Halston I thought I might actually ask Mom to buy for me, and the other was this amazing zebra-print Patrick Kelly gown that looked like something someone would wear in an opera but that I couldn't resist trying on for the fun of it, though I was afraid I was too bony to pull it off.

But because of the cannolis, my stomach was all pooched out so that the clingy Halston looked just plain embarrassing, but the Patrick Kelly fit perfectly. The skirt was so big I had to ease out of the dressing room sideways, and the dress itself was so spectacular that as I stood in front of the mirror, Desi straightening the bodice and flouncing out the ruffles, everyone in the store turned to look.

And kept looking.

I smiled into the mirror, and stood up straighter.

Suddenly a woman stepped forward, a woman who was maybe my mom's age, but who was nearly as thin as me, wearing a baby-doll top and high-heeled pink sandals and a pair of those bleached and torn $300 jeans. Her hair was very black and very straight, as if she'd just come from a blowout. The closer she got, the older she looked.

"Have you ever thought of modeling?" she said, holding a card out to me.

I felt myself blush. "I couldn't," I said. "I mean, I'm from Eagle River, Wisconsin."

Desi took the card and said, "She might be interested."

The woman looked at Desi in a way that finally made me understand what it means to "look down your nose" at somebody. She raised her eyebrows, and turned back to me.

"I'm Raquel Gross of Awesome Models," she said, "and you're the kind of girl we might be interested in."

"Wow," I said. "I mean, is this a joke?"

I laughed and turned to Desi, expecting her to laugh right back. As long as I could remember, everyone had always made fun of the way I looked, to the point where they did it right in front of me. I was so tall, so skinny, so gawky and weird-looking, they figured, if I was any kind of cool I'd be able to laugh about it myself. And I had, I had even when it hurt.

But Desi wasn't laughing. She wouldn't even meet my eye. Instead she was alternately looking seriously at Raquel and peering down at the business card.

"Awesome Models," she said. "I've read about you. Don't you represent Fiona and Fernanda?"

Raquel nodded, not taking her eyes off me. "We represent all the hottest girls working today: Kaylee, Christiana, Ludovica, My Lan. And don't tell anybody"—here Raquel leaned closer and spoke in a stage whisper—"but we just signed Tatiana."

I laughed again. Who was I going to tell? Tom? All Tom was interested in was fish, football, and sex. Oh my gosh: Tom. I was supposed to call him when we arrived, and I'd completely forgotten. I guessed if he got worried and called the hotel, Mom would fill him in. I'd call him when I got back to the room, before I went to sleep, to tell him I loved him and missed him, at least when I had a second to think about him.

When I refocused, I saw that Desi was nodding vigorously, her mouth open. "Oh my God—Tatiana," she was saying. "She's amazing. But I've read that she's really difficult. How did you manage to sign her?"

Finally Raquel turned to Desi, obviously impressed that she had the inside scoop. "We can offer girls the most comprehensive security, financial as well as emotional, along with complete benefits and the most creative work with the best photographers in the world. Everybody wants to sign with us."

Desi nodded, examining the card again. "And so you're offering all this amazing stuff to Amanda?"

"I'm offering Amanda the *opportunity* to be *considered* by Awesome Models," Raquel said. "I'd like to send her for some test shots with one of our top photographers, see whether she really has what it takes to make it in the New York modeling world."

"I don't have what it takes," I said. "Besides, I don't want to move to New York. I'm going to marry Tom."

"You're engaged?" cried Desi, her eye darting to my ring finger.

"Not officially, but I will be, as soon as I get back home, right after I turn eighteen. We're going to get married in September."

"But you have such *fabulous* cheekbones," Raquel said. "And those lips. That height. I even adore your little pouch of a stomach."

"That's the cannolis," I mumbled.

"Maybe you should think about this," said Desi. "I mean, September is three months away."

"If we sign you, we'd pay you a twenty-thousand-dollar signing bonus right away and guarantee you a hundred thousand dollars in income in your first year. That's minimum; it could be much more. We'd set you up in an apartment, pay all your expenses. Physical trainer, clothing allowance, expense account . . ."

But my brain was still stuck on the signing bonus. Tom's dream was to buy a fishing boat. If he had his own boat, he could guide whole parties fishing out on the lakes, not just individual clients. That could mean four or six or eight times as much income for him, for *us*. Just imagining the look on his face was priceless.

"So this twenty thousand dollars," I said. "I'd get this up front, immediately?"

Raquel nodded. "But first you have to do the test shots. I'd send you to Alex Pradels, who's a fabulous photographer. If those pictures worked out, and if you signed with us, then you'd get the twenty thousand dollars."

"Twenty-five," said Desi.

"What?" said Raquel.

"We want twenty-five as a signing bonus, and another

twenty-five if Amanda's income in the first six months exceeds fifty thousand dollars."

"What are you, her agent?" Raquel asked.

"Yes," Desi said, at the same moment I said, "No."

I looked at Desi. What the heck? This was all pretend anyway. And I certainly had no idea what I was doing. "Okay, yes," I said.

"We're open to negotiating the terms," said Raquel, "depending on the results of the shoot."

"And I'm assuming," said Desi, "that you cover all the expenses of the shoot, and that Amanda is entitled to prints even if we don't come to an agreement."

Raquel hesitated only a moment before nodding.

Desi turned to me. "You should do it," she said. "Alex Pradels is one of the best. It'll be fun. At the very least, you'll get a great picture to put in the newspaper when you announce your engagement."

That sounded good, though I still couldn't imagine that this was something that in any way was going to become real—and if it did, that it was anything I'd ever want to do. Though I sure would love to be able to buy Tom that boat.

"What if I want to quit?" I blurted.

Desi glared at me. I knew she would have liked the opportunity to make my question prettier. But then I was afraid I'd get a prettier answer, which might not necessarily be as true.

Raquel laughed and squeezed my arm. "This isn't slavery you're signing up for," she assured me. "It's the most glamorous job in the world! All you have to worry about is staying as beautiful as you already are, and let me take care of the rest."

But somehow, instead of calming my fears or getting me excited about the possibilities, she was only making me more nervous. It was like when it hits you that the big fish on your line probably has teeth.

two

*T*here was a moment when I could have run, when I wanted to run. I was sitting in front of the makeup mirror in Alex Pradels's studio, staring at my reflection. Someone I didn't know stared back at me. She had eyelashes like spider legs, and skin made of latex, and a mouth that looked like somebody had socked her and then rubbed raspberries all around for good measure. Her hair was ratted and teased and sprayed; it felt like cotton candy, the kind that's been hardening inside a plastic bag for months.

This was the result of two hours of hard work by a British makeup artist who wore no makeup herself and refused to meet my eye, and a hairdresser named Glenn, who looked pretty much like a guy except he was wearing high heels, and I don't mean cowboy boots.

Out in the studio, Alex and his young Asian assistant, who looked like she was in grade school, were setting up backdrops and carting around lights and fiddling with the music, alternating it between loud and louder. Every once in a while, Alex, who looked like the guy who played Julia Roberts's best friend in that old movie *My Best Friend's Wedding,* but who was not at all a nice person, would pop his head in and look me over as if I were a friend's pet that he'd promised, against his will, to take in for grooming.

"How's she coming along?" he'd ask the makeup artist or hairdresser, or the stylist who was wedging me into one ridiculous piece of clothing after another. The one part of this experience I'd been really excited about was getting to wear the kind of fabulous designer clothes I'd been drooling over in the pages of magazines, but these clothes were from the bizarre-o side of fashion: shirts with sleeves like wings and skirts with snakelike pieces of fabric hanging from them, coats made of rubber and pants with snakeskin laces down the sides.

"Fabulous," they all said.

No one asked me, but if they had, I would have told them I thought I looked like something in a field you really did not want to step in. Ordinarily I did not consider myself the least bit beautiful, but compared to this mess, I was Miss Wisconsin before I even brushed my teeth.

Hating the way I looked wasn't the only problem. It was my birthday. When Raquel and my mom tried to schedule this sitting, I said I'd do it any day but my birthday—and then this turned out to be the only day when all the other people could be there. Mom talked me into it, told me it would make a memorable way to spend my eighteenth birthday. Even Tom said I should do it, though he went silent when I told him that if it worked out I could buy him the boat. He wouldn't admit it, but I guess that was an offense to his male ego. And now this was turning out to be even more dismal than I thought it was going to be.

Suddenly I realized I was alone in the dressing room. The red-painted door that opened to the stairs that led one flight down to the street was to my left, slightly ajar. I could even see a sliver of daylight through the glass door at the bottom of the stairs. I could stand up, walk down the stairs, push my way outside, find a phone booth, call Mom back in the studio to let her know I was gone.

I peeked into the studio, where Mom was camped by the buffet table, helping herself from the mountain of bagels that had gone otherwise untouched. Glenn and the makeup artist were sniggering in the corner. The stylist looked to be licking the edge of a piece of chocolate while staring vacantly toward strobe lights kind of like the ones they'd had at the Northland Pines prom, which kept popping off as Alex took test shots of the assistant.

I could go. They'd never notice—or at least not until I'd made a clean escape. Shouldn't a person do exactly what she wanted on her birthday, especially on her eighteenth birthday?

It wouldn't take a minute. I'd scrub my face with soap and water and then I'd stick my head under the faucet. I'd pull on one of my refashioned T-shirt dresses, slip on my flip-flops, and I'd be history.

And that's just what happened, until the part where I pushed open the red door and started to step out into the hallway, the stairs just ahead, when something stopped me. It was my mom's voice. She hadn't spotted me; she wasn't calling me or anything. No, she was doing something far more alarming. She was speaking French.

At first I thought maybe I was mistaken. As far as I knew, my mom spoke not a word of French or any other language besides English. Maybe it was Makeup Woman or Child Assistant who was chattering away in French with Alex. But no, I'd taken enough French in high school to detect a distinct Wisconsin accent in such telltale words as *beaucoup* and *croissant*.

Croissant was the one French word I'd heard Mom say, because she made them for the Sunday morning crowd at the pie shop. She'd always mispronounced the word the same way everyone else in Eagle River did: *croyzent*. And *croyzent* was exactly what she said now. There was an awkward silence, as if someone had farted loudly, and then Alex corrected her, "It's *kwa-sant*, madame."

"Oh God," Mom tittered. "Saying it that way would make me feel like I was putting on airs."

"Croyzent," I heard Glenn say. "Un-fucking-believable."

"I don't know why Raquel lets these girls drag their entire families in here," sniffed the makeup artist.

That was it. I stormed into the studio.

"Come on, Mom," I said. "We're leaving."

Mom looked up at me, her mouth open.

"You can't let these hoity-toity skeeveballs talk to you like that. Let's get out of here."

"One hundred fucking dollars of product, down the drain," huffed Glenn.

"I'm still billing Awesome," said the makeup artist. "Double."

Mom kept sitting there, so I walked over and tugged her up. "Let's go, Mom," I said, more gently now.

"Just a second," said Alex, walking over to me.

I flinched, thinking he was going to grab my arm, or yell at me about how I couldn't do this. But instead he brushed a piece of wet hair back from where it had been plastered to my face and touched—so lightly my whole body tingled—the edge of my now bare lip.

"*Magnifique*," he whispered, turning to Mom. "*N'est-ce pas, Maman?*"

"I always tell her she's beautiful just the way she is," said Mom, smiling beatifically.

Alex clapped his hands. "We will shoot the pictures like this, au naturel."

I froze. "But I told you," I said. "I'm leaving."

He froze. He had the ability to freeze in a much more meaningful way than I did. "But you cannot leave," he said finally. "This is the moment of your life. Come, everyone. We begin."

He moved toward his camera and his assistant scurried to turn on the lights. The rest of us stayed where we were.

"She'll look totally washed out," Makeup Woman said.

"Let me at least blow her dry," said Glenn.

"No one touches me," I said, backing toward the door.

"The rest of you can leave," said Alex. "I'm sorry, but you too, Maman. We need nothing but the camera and the girl." He laughed lightly. "And of course, the artist."

"No way," I said, crossing my arms tightly over my chest.

"Ah, the princess has further objections. What's the problem now?"

"I don't want to be alone with you," I told him.

He opened his mouth but apparently decided not to say what he was going to say, instead raising his arm into the air and actually—catch this—snapping his fingers. "All right, Yuki stays," he said. "Everyone else, clear the room. We begin."

Here's what I would say: It wasn't as horrible as I was afraid it was going to be, mostly because I just stood there, doing nothing, or sat there, doing nothing, or let myself flop over the stool, doing nothing, and "the artist" snapped away. For a while he tried to say those ridiculous things that you see in every TV movie about models—"You're beautiful, baby!"—until I told him, "Won't you please be quiet, please."

Then he cranked up the music and I stood or sat there and thought about what I was going to eat for dinner tonight, at the restaurant under the Brooklyn Bridge, the one with the amazing view of all New York, that Mom was taking me to. Now that it was my birthday, I technically could tell her about me and Tom. I also planned to ask Mom how she learned to speak French, and why she'd kept this ability hidden from me.

Mulling all this over, I definitely was not smiling or looking at the camera. The so-called artist didn't seem to care.

These pictures were definitely going to suck. That realization, at least, brought a little smile to my lips.

· · ·

"It sucked, Mom."

We were sitting in the most beautiful place I had ever been in my entire life. The restaurant itself was all golden and glittery, with crystal chandeliers and candles on every table, reflected in the windows that looked out on the river and the lit-up buildings *and* on the lights of the buildings reflected in the river. It felt magical, being there, like I'd always imagined the prince's palace felt to Cinderella. I wanted to feel like Cinderella myself, transformed by turning eighteen in this awesome place. We'd just finished eating and I'd decided that over dessert I was going to tell Mom about me and Tom. All through dinner I'd avoided talking about the photo shoot, but now I wanted to leave it behind in the land of before: before my real adult life started and I had the power to make sure only good things happened to me. After tonight I'd marry Tom and study art and literature at Nicolet College in Rhinelander and maybe open a vintage clothing store in Eagle River. But first there was one thing I had to know.

"I hated it and I never want to talk about it again," I told Mom. "But you have to tell me why you never let on that you spoke French."

Mom hesitated, then refilled her wineglass, even splashing a little into mine. Then she took a big gulp, which wasn't like her. She was more an eater than a drinker.

"I'm sure you knew I spoke French," Mom said, not looking at me. "It's not like it was any big secret."

Mom was a terrible liar. Even a little fib, like telling a customer the apple pie would be ready in five minutes when it was really going to be more like seven, she could hardly pull off. In fact, on the rare occasion when she attempted it, she'd start babbling and end up telling way more truth than anybody wanted to hear.

"I mean," she said now, "I wasn't *trying* to keep it a secret. It's not like anybody *French* ever comes to Eagle River. And if they did, and they came into the pie shop, and they couldn't speak a word of English and they couldn't even *point,* for goodness' sake, and so instead they said something like, '*Je voudrais une tarte aux pommes,*' which means they wanted an apple pie...."

"I know what it means, Mom," I interrupted. "I took French all through high school, remember? I'd walk around the house memorizing these stupid dialogues, and you never once offered to practice with me, or showed any sign that you had any clue what I was mumbling about."

The dessert arrived and Mom totally ignored it, instead refilling her wineglass before the waiter was able to rush over. This was a very alarming sign.

"I was afraid if you knew I could speak French you'd start asking questions," Mom said, letting out such a huge breath of air that afterward she sat slumped on her chair like a deflated balloon.

The windows and the view were behind her—she'd insisted that as the birthday girl I look out on the city—and through the first part of the evening she'd seemed like an element of the splendor: my loving mom, so sweet and generous she'd brought me to this amazing place, the brightest star in the universe before me. But now she seemed not only oblivious to the beauty behind her but at war with it, dark and disturbed, denying all the light.

"What are you talking about, Mom?"

She sighed again and finally looked me in the eye. "I didn't see any reason you'd ever have to know."

"Know *what*, for land's sake?"

"I learned to speak French from your father, Amanda. Oh sure, I took it in high school, but I didn't really *get* it until I met your father and we started speaking it together. I mean, that's *all* we spoke for those three months. . . ."

I was even more stumped than I'd been before. My dad, Duke, was a lot like Tom: He didn't do too much talking in any language. And I knew he'd never been much for school, preferring, as he put it, to "learn from the fish."

"*Dad* speaks French?"

It was Mom's turn to look confused for a moment, and then she actually laughed. "Oh, not Duke. No no no no, not Duke. I mean your real father. Your biological father."

I stared at her. People had always said, from the time I was the littlest girl, how much I looked like my dad—like Duke. It was partly because Mom was so heavy and I was so skinny; no one in Eagle River could even imagine what she'd looked like when she was modeling, or see the resemblance between her and me. But I knew from looking at pictures of her when she was young and thin that I looked much more like her than like Dad, though it made him so happy when people said it.

Now I felt like not only did I not know what Mom was talking about, I didn't know Mom. And my dad wasn't my dad. I felt like I was going to throw up all over the starched tablecloth.

"Am I adopted?" I said, practically choking on the words. "Are you my real mother?"

"Of *course* I'm your real mother," she said, her voice rising to that hysterical pitch I knew from the day the pie shop was robbed, or when Grandma died. "When I saw you all done up for that shoot today, it took me back to my own modeling days. I felt like I was looking in the mirror. And meeting Alex, being in that studio, speaking French again—it just all came flooding back."

"*What* came flooding back? You better tell me the truth now, Mom, and I mean the whole truth."

Here it is: She'd been to New York before. That's why she started crying when we first saw the city. She'd come here when she was eighteen, my age, to model. Very quickly, she'd met a photographer, a Frenchman, and they'd fallen in love. Or at least *she'd* fallen in love. He went to France for a visit, and while he was gone she found out he was married. At about the same time she discovered she was pregnant. With me. She went back to Eagle River, where my father, I mean Duke, had been her high school boyfriend. She told him everything, and he wanted to marry her anyway. They agreed that he would claim me as his own. No one would ever have to know who my real father was.

"So why are you telling me now?" I asked her. I was more furious than I'd ever been in my entire life, partly for her having lied to me for all these years, and partly for her now spilling the truth.

"Seeing you there today at that shoot, so beautiful, such a natural, I thought: If you're going to be in modeling, you've got to know the truth. You might meet your father, you might even work with him, and it's wrong if you don't know who he is. His name is Jean-Pierre Renaud; he's quite well-known. I thought you'd stay in Eagle River your whole life. . . ."

"I just told you I am *not* going to be 'in modeling,'" I said, slamming my hands down so hard on the table that the silverware and the crystal glasses leaped into the air, Mom's wine toppling and draining like blood across the tablecloth.

"I think that's a mistake," Mom said, fumbling to right her glass, her face so red it seemed like she was about to start sobbing—though at that moment I couldn't have cared less. "Though I'd love it if you were with me in Eagle River. . . ."

"I don't know what I'm going to do," I said, staggering to my feet, jostling the table again so that the flames of the candles quaked in the reflection in the window. I couldn't see the city anymore; all I could see was myself, enormous, looming over Mom.

"All I know," I told her, "is that I don't want to be with you."

. . .

What I did want to do, and why I couldn't do it:

1. Sit down in a dark corner and cry. Reason I couldn't do: Might get raped and murdered in all available dark corners.

2. Get in a taxi or even on the subway and go to Desi's house. But I didn't have any money because I was wearing my sari, which naturally had no pockets and which didn't go with any of my purses so I'd asked Mom to carry my wallet.

3. Talk to Tom. But no cell phone, no money to use pay phone.

4. Go back to hotel. Did not want to see Mom.

So I just started walking. It became apparent pretty quickly that I could either continue walking along the waterfront, veer off into darkest Brooklyn, or head onto the Brooklyn Bridge itself. At least the bridge was easy to find: All I had to do was look up, and keep walking toward the majestic span. In the cab on the way over here, I'd seen people walking and jogging—including families, women alone, even old people—along the bridge's official walkway. I'd thought at the time that it looked like a really fun thing to do and tried to calculate whether I'd be able to squeeze it in before our plane left for Wisconsin tomorrow night. Now I had my answer.

It was a warm night and there were even more people on the walkway now than there had been before. With all the people around, I was less afraid walking by myself there than I was on my own street in Eagle River at this time of night, which would be completely deserted. It was an amazing feeling being there, like walking on a rainbow over heaven.

But no matter how transcendent the setting, I wasn't able to lose myself to the experience of being there. There were too many voices banging around in my head. How could my mom have lied to me all those years? Did Dad—I mean Duke—really love me, or was he always thinking of me underneath as something tainted? And who was my real father, this Jean-Pierre whoever? Was it *him* that I looked like? Would I ever meet him? Did I *want* to?

When I reached the Manhattan end of the bridge, I knew what I was going to do. I'd been to Desi's apartment once, when she wanted to change her shoes. Now I headed there. Or I should say I *tried* to head there, but in the maze of downtown streets, all with names instead of numbers, it was next to impossible to figure out which way to go. My only guiding light was the Empire State Building—that was north. But the streets on the Manhattan side of the bridge, around the big court and government buildings, were dark and deserted, and the few people I saw, people in suits hurrying to the subway after a late night at the office, ignored my request for directions.

I finally sank onto a park bench near City Hall and started crying, because I was lost in every way. I closed my eyes and tried to will myself out of this whole huge mess back into Tom's arms. If only I'd never come to New York, had stayed in Wisconsin and married Tom. But that wouldn't have made any difference, I reminded myself. Even if I'd never found out about my real French father, it still would have been true.

I didn't even notice that a homeless person had sat down beside me until she slid closer and held out a McDonald's napkin, which I gratefully took.

"Man trouble?" she asked.

"No," I sobbed. "My mother lied to me. And I'm not who I thought I was."

"I'm not who I thought I was either," she said.

"And I'm trying to get to my friend Desi's apartment," I told her, "but I can't find my way."

This she could help me with, giving me amazingly detailed directions that included the kind of bark on a tree and the color of a sidewalk grate. I wished I could give her some money or some food, but that night I had even less than she did.

Once I made it to the crowded streets of Chinatown and Little Italy, and then to the cool part of the Lower East Side, there were at least lots of people to point the way. By the time I reached Desi's building, which stood between a vacant lot and a tenement where guys lounged on the front steps smoking something highly illegal, my feet were blistered and bleeding and it was so late my heart was pounding in fear as well as exhaustion. I was relieved when I rang the bell downstairs that she was home and buzzed me in immediately, before I had a chance to get killed. I moved as quickly as I could through the dark hallways of her building, definitely a less privileged side of New York than the rich restaurant where I'd so recently been gorging myself on a dinner that might have fed one of Desi's neighbors for a week.

The last time I'd been to Desi's apartment had been in the middle of a weekday and nobody was around, but tonight it was packed with people, the stereo going, the TV blaring, guys in baseball caps and gold chains sprawled on the couch, kids running screaming across the rug, while in the kitchen Desi's mom was frying eggplant. Desi herself stood serenely in the middle of all the chaos, pinning vintage fabric on a mannequin.

"Which ones are your brothers and sisters?" I asked Desi.

"They all are," she said, smiling slightly. "Except Chico, the guy in the Yankees cap. He's my cousin."

"Wow," I said.

I'd never seen a family that looked more alike in more unusual a way. Desi's mom was the same size and shape as Desi—tiny and round—but a completely different color, with pale red hair and even paler freckled skin. The room was filled with other people who all had the same basic shape, but with a range of skin tones, from one blonde little girl to a boy with skin the warm color of a chestnut, with Desi and the two guys on the couch somewhere in between.

"So I thought you were out to dinner with your mom?" Desi said.

That's when I burst into tears again.

She maneuvered me into her tiny bedroom, where I had to lift my legs up onto the bed to make room for Desi to shut the door.

"Tell me," she said, sitting down on the bed with me and taking my hands.

So I told her. I told her everything my mom had told me, how I'd felt, what I'd thought on my walk across the bridge and through the streets of Lower Manhattan. When I finished, there was a long pause before Desi spoke.

"Is that it?" she said finally.

I nodded, sniffing back tears.

"That's all?" she asked again.

Again I nodded.

"But what's the big deal?" she said.

I blinked, squeezing out two more fat tears. I thought Desi and I were soulmates. I couldn't believe I had to explain this to her.

"I've never met my father," I said. "I don't even know what he looks like, what kind of person he is."

Desi shrugged. "So I've never met my father either. Did you get a look around out there? All five of us have different fathers and we haven't met any of them. It doesn't mean we're any less happy. We're probably *more* happy. The guys were probably bums, or my mom would have kept them around."

"Yeah, but my mom lied to me. It's like my whole life is a lie. I don't even know who I am anymore."

Desi considered this. "Lying is no good," she said.

"I'm so mad at my mother, I never want to see her again."

"You don't mean that."

"I do mean it. I hate her."

"Oh, come on, Amanda. She's a good mother. Maybe she made this one mistake but . . ."

"I can't see her tonight," I told Desi. "Can I stay here? I mean, I know you don't have much room but . . ."

"If you don't mind squeezing into this bed with me," said Desi. "I'll call the hotel so your mom doesn't worry. You'll feel different in the morning."

· · ·

In the morning, I was still mad. I still felt as if my life had been turned inside out. But I was ready to talk to Mom about it.

To my astonishment, when I called her at the hotel she answered the phone with the cheeriest of voices, as if she'd just come from her Monday afternoon poker game, where she and her girlfriends were known to mix themselves a few cosmos and pretend they were characters in some North Woods version of *Sex and the City: Sex and the Pine Trees.*

"I am so angry at you," I snarled, going for the kind of slap that would wipe the smile I could tell was on her face right *off*.

But Mom was not to be deterred. "Oh, I know, dear," she said, trying to sound concerned and contrite. "And I'm really sorry I sprang that on you like that, and that I ruined your birthday, and upset you so much. But the most exciting thing has happened. That woman from the modeling agency, Raquel, has called about fifty times. Apparently the pictures Alex took of you yesterday are *amazing*—that's the word she used—and they're ready to sign you right away. This morning. Each time she calls she keeps offering more money!"

"Mom, what are you *talking* about? We're in *crisis* here. This thing about my father is a lot more important than any stupid modeling contract."

"I wouldn't say that," Mom said. "Oh, I know it's important, but we have a whole lifetime to work this out. But your big chance for a career is here and now. We have to set all these other problems aside and think about that."

"I can't just set these problems aside so easily," I told her. "And I don't want to be a model. I want to marry Tom."

There. I'd finally struck her silent. So silent that I began to fear the line had gone dead and ventured, "Mom?"

"I'm here," Mom said. "Oh, Amanda. It isn't that I don't like Tom. He's a wonderful young man. He reminds me of your father—I mean of Duke. But you have a chance at something so much more than that. This would be an opportunity for you to travel the world and make more money in a few years than Tom's going to make in a lifetime as a fishing guide. And if you give the modeling a shot and you and Tom still want to be together, then you can marry him."

I didn't say anything. I didn't want to give her the benefit of knowing she was making a good point.

"Maybe Tom wouldn't want to marry a girl who'd lived in New York and worked as some hot-ass model," I said finally. I said it to keep arguing with Mom, but once it was out of my mouth I realized that was what I was really afraid of.

"Then maybe he's not the man for you," Mom said quietly.

I was nervous I was about to start liking her again when she said the thing that tipped me over the edge.

"Listen, honey, I just want the best for you," she said. "I know what it's like to settle down in Eagle River at a young age, to realize this is it, and I wish I'd had the chance you have, to go further as a model, to go to Europe . . ."

"But you couldn't because you got pregnant with me."

Stunned silence.

"That's the real truth, isn't it, Mom?" I said, ready to blast her now. "Getting pregnant with me forced you to go back to Eagle River, forced you into this life you never wanted. That's why you got so *fat*. Because I ruined your life."

I slammed down the phone and sucked air in and out of my lungs so hard I felt like I was going to faint. There was no way now that I was going back to Eagle River, no way I was going to speak to my mother ever again. This avalanche of truth had forced me into my own choice, but it wasn't the same one my mom had made.

I felt a pang thinking of my dad, I mean Duke, and wished I could talk to him about this tangle of news and feelings. But he'd never been good at talking on the phone, even about something unpressured like the weather. And if I called him, then he'd immediately tell Mom, and they'd team up to try and drag me back to Wisconsin.

The only thing left for me to do was call Tom, tell him everything that had happened, ask him what he thought about my signing the modeling contract and staying in New York, just for now, just long enough for me to make enough money for us to get married and buy a house and for me never to have to work at the House O' Pies or rely on my mother for anything ever again.

Tom answered with far more words than he usually strung together at one time. "You don't want to know what I think; you want my permission," he said. "But that's something you don't need. You should do what you want to do, Amanda. And when you're done doing it, I'll be here waiting."

three

*H*ere are the first things I noticed about Raquel Gross's office:

1. Everything that wasn't glass was steel.

2. Everything that wasn't hard—i.e. glass or steel—was red.

3. The phone and the computer were as thin and shiny as the blade of a knife.

4. All the books on the bookshelves were covered with white paper, their titles hand-printed on the spines in black ink.

5. Raquel herself was completely outfitted in black (her clothes), steel and glass (her jewelry), except her mouth was the same bright red as the office accents.

As soon as she saw me, Raquel Gross clicked her switchblade phone closed as if there hadn't been anyone on the other end and hurried around her glass and steel desk to enfold me in a huge embrace. No one had ever hugged me that long and hard except my mom and Tom, and they don't count for various reasons. I mean no one who barely knew me.

"I am *so excited*," she said, rocking me back and forth.

"Me too," I tried to say, though she was holding me so tight it came out as "Mmm-tuh."

"I knew I was right," she said, pushing me away so she could look at me, but still not letting go. "I know these things. That's why I am what I am."

"Uh-huh," I said, like I did when Tom started going on about the feeding habits of the Great Northern.

"You . . . are . . . going . . . to . . . be . . . a . . . star," she said, separating the words like that.

"Wow."

"I'm so glad you decided to sign," she said, bustling back to her side of the desk and motioning for me to sit. "That is *so* the right decision. I mean, 'Should I pursue a fabulous modeling career or do nothing in nowheresville?' Duh!"

When I didn't laugh, she cleared her throat and shuffled through the papers in front of her.

"Where's your manager?" she asked.

"My . . . uh . . ." I stumbled, unsure how to explain.

Desi had offered to come along to Raquel's. But I felt, after the mess with Mom, that I wanted to do this on my own. Completely on my own, with no lies, nothing hidden.

"Desi and I are still friends," I said, "but we've parted ways on the managing thing."

The corners of Raquel's mouth turned up in a smile as quick as a blink.

"All right," she said, pushing the first thick stack of papers toward me. "Initial here and here and here, and sign here, and, let me see, here."

I picked up the document, thick and dense as a history paper, except neater, and started reading.

"What are you doing?" Raquel said.

"I'm reading it."

She snapped her scarlet-tipped fingers in the air. "This is New York!" she cried. "People do things fast here! They don't read their contracts."

I hesitated. "Maybe I should have my mom look at this."

Although I would rather have kissed that jerk Alex Pradels than actually bring my mom into this deal. I hadn't even told her I'd decided to come here, to sign the contract. I was an adult now, free to make my own decisions. But I wished I could show the contract at least to Desi before signing it.

Raquel narrowed her eyes at me. "I thought you turned eighteen yesterday. Are you sure you're legally responsible to sign this?"

"Of course," I said, feeling the heat rise to my cheeks.

"Maybe you better let me have a look at your driver's license."

My face now blazing, the way it does when you get stopped by a cop even when you know you were going the speed limit, I fished the license out of my wallet—Desi had gotten my stuff from Mom—and handed it to her. Then, while she was squinting down at it, moving her lips in an effort to do the math, I scribbled my initials and name across the contract before she could change her mind. Finally satisfied, she slid the rest of the copies across the desk to me to sign.

When I was finished, Raquel tapped the papers into a neat stack and said, "Now I'll take you to your apartment."

"But I don't have an apartment."

She laughed lightly in a way that told me she didn't think anything was funny.

"I mean the apartment we rent on your behalf," she said. "It's right in clause thirty-seven of the contract."

"Wow," I said.

"Yeah," Raquel said. "Wow. Tomorrow, you have your first go-see—that's like an audition, but for models. But now I'll take you up to your place so you can get settled in."

. . .

When Raquel opened the door to my new apartment, I was shocked to see the place was so dense with smoke it looked like the prom when the band turned on the fog machine, and it smelled like Winkler's Tavern late on a cold Saturday night. All the windows were shut because the air conditioner was blasting. Through the mist I could just make out the long, thin figure of a beautiful girl reclining on the couch. Reclining on the couch and, of course, smoking.

"Tatiana!" cried Raquel, moving toward the couch as if to embrace the reclining figure, but then apparently changing her mind and flopping into a hard-looking chair, lighting up herself. "What are you doing inside on such a beautiful day?"

Tatiana yawned widely and resumed puffing. "Day is shit," she growled finally.

"Fresh air is good for you," Raquel said, wagging her finger. "As long as you wear lots of sunscreen."

She turned around toward me then and expelled an energetic gust of smoke, which left her mouth free to break into a wide smile. "See how well I take care of you girls?" she said. "I should have children. Don't you think I'd be a great mother?"

I'd always thought I had a great mother, who cooked me three hot meals a day and brushed my hair every night and bought me every single thing I wanted for Christmas. But look where that ended up: with betrayal. Maybe Raquel's brand of mothering would be better.

"All I need is the man," she said.

"Men are swine," said Tatiana.

"Not all men," I said, thinking of Tom. "Some men are more like . . . whisky jacks."

This seemed to perk up Tatiana.

"Ha!" she cried. "Men are whisky-jacking swine!"

"The whisky jack is a bird," I told her. "A forest bird. It's big and gentle like a Great Dane, and also sweet and unafraid, and just likes to hang around the same place all the time."

There was a pair of whisky jacks in the forest on the island in Big Secret Lake where Tom and I camped every year. The male was so accustomed to Tom, who was always on that lake, that it sometimes perched on his shoulder when he was fishing by himself. Those two were so much alike,

I thought of the whisky jack as an animal manifestation of Tom's soul.

"That doesn't sound like any of the men I know in New York," said Raquel, "except maybe my doorman, and I don't want to date him."

"There are a lot of men like that where I come from," I said.

"Maybe that's what I need," Raquel said, "a big strong strapping country boy, bursting with sperm. Do you know someone like that you could introduce me to?"

I surveyed her, with her makeup and her black clothes and her cigarette. It was hard to imagine any of the boys I knew at school wanting to go out with her, or ever coming to New York to find out. It was even harder to imagine her kicking it in Eagle River. But I didn't want to just say no.

Ten Things to Say When You Can't Say No

1. I'll think about it.
2. Is that the phone ringing?
3. You have something weird in your teeth.
4. You don't really want that.
5. I wouldn't do that to you.
6. Oh my Gosh, look at the time.
7. Oh my Gosh, I think I'm going to be sick.
8. Your question reminds me of a really funny story.
9. I'll ask my mom/my neighbor/my boyfriend.
10. Sure.

Unfortunately I picked option number 10.

"Great!" Raquel said. "Oooh, a real macho man. But he

has to be someone I won't be embarrassed to take to Blue Fin or WD50. And he absolutely must like the ballet. That's nonnegotiable."

I looked away from Raquel so I wouldn't burst out laughing and my gaze landed on Tatiana's. We exchanged the tiniest flicker of a smile, which prompted an equally tiny flicker of hope in my heart.

"Amanda is from northern Wisconsin," Raquel explained to Tatiana. "That's something like the Ukraine, except in America."

"Like Ukraine?" Tatiana asked, a smile still playing at the edges of her fabulous lips. "Is shit place?"

"No, it's beautiful," I said, hugging my straw bag to my chest and thinking of the way Big Secret sparkled in the summer sun.

Raquel stubbed out her cigarette and got to her feet. "I've got to consult my psychic about this. And my therapist. I've got this weird, tingly feeling that this mountain man, whoever he is, is going to be the father of my baby."

"There aren't really any mountains in northern Wisconsin," I said.

Raquel looked at me as if I might be joking. Then she commenced brushing nonexistent lint from her black clothing. "Mountains, forests, whatever," she said. "Don't you think I'll be a fabulous mom? Come on, Tatiana, I've got to take you to an appointment."

Tatiana groaned loudly. "Is crap of dawn!"

"That's *crack* of dawn, and no, in fact, it is the *afternoon*, and as you know, the agency rule is up at six and proceed immediately to the gym, which you have obviously skipped today. That is unacceptable, especially after yesterday's screw-up. As Tatiana should know, Amanda, the other rules are lights out at ten, keep the place neat, and no drinking, drugs, men, or smoking."

Behind Raquel's back, Tatiana grinned at me and then crossed her eyes and stuck out her tongue. I couldn't help it, I grinned back, which Raquel interpreted as my not really taking her seriously.

"We're obviously lenient on the smoking rule, because it's good for your figure," she explained. "And we're between maids at this place. But otherwise we're very serious about our rules. And if you break them"—here she leveled a severe look at Tatiana—"you could be cut by the agency."

Raquel then took a yellow silk envelope fat with money from her black reptile purse and handed me ten pristine twenty-dollar bills, a tiny cell phone, and a key, golden, to the apartment. On the back of one of her business cards, she scribbled a name and address.

"First thing in the morning, you're going to *Vogue*. More rules: Show up on time, be polite, and don't express any opinions. Remember, you're under contract now. Any violations and your career is over."

· · ·

The first thing I did after Raquel and Tatiana left the apartment was open all the windows. That made it hot and noisy and smelly from traffic fumes and street smells, but at least it got some of the smoke out. Then I found an unopened box of trash bags and filled several of those with empty beer bottles, champagne bottles, vodka bottles, and water bottles, and hauled them downstairs. Then I hung up the dozens of items of clothing littered around the apartment. Then I wiped everything down with a T-shirt and then I vacuumed.

Then I flopped down exhausted on one of the twin beds in the apartment's only bedroom, thinking this is what my mom must feel like a lot of the time. I hadn't let myself think about my mom all day, and now that I had it felt like somebody had plunged a sharp instrument into my chest and hooked it around my heart. I imagined Mom sitting in the room at the Holiday Inn, frantic with worry, overdue to leave for the flight for Wisconsin and having no idea whether she should go. Retrieving the cell phone Raquel had given me, I dialed the number of Mom's big old cell phone. She let out a sob when she heard my voice.

"Thank God you're safe," she said.

"I'm safe, Mom." I had to work to keep my voice steady and cool. With my mom, all my emotions were always right out there for her to sort through and mop up. But I couldn't do that anymore. I was a grown-up now.

"I signed the modeling contract," I told her.

She was silent.

"You were right," I said. "It is an amazing opportunity. I've already got an apartment, a fabulous apartment, and I'll be staying in New York."

"What about Tom?" Mom finally managed to say.

"We've talked it over. He thinks I should go for it."

"So the flight tonight . . ." Mom said. "Your ticket . . ."

"I'll give you the money for it," I told her breezily. "But you better hurry up if you're going to get to the airport. I'll be in touch."

And then I hung up, before I could change my mind.

four

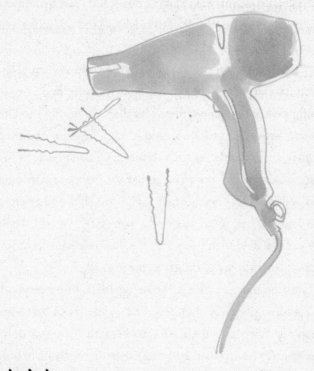

When my alarm went off at six the next morning, it was still dark outside and Tatiana was not in her bed. Good thing I'd given up waiting up for her and gone to sleep at ten fifteen, after soothing my loneliness with a long talk on the phone with Desi. Thank God for Desi: I felt like I could tell her anything, or just giggle on the phone with her talking about nothing important, but feel like I had a friend who understood me and cared about me no matter what.

Everything looked brighter this morning, though, figuratively and literally. The windows were still wide open and the air smelled fresh, like New York had taken a shower while I was asleep. The sun was beaming down and I saw that indeed it had rained in the middle of the night; all the sidewalks were wet and glistening.

I'd been planning to take a cab to the address Raquel had given me but on the spur of the moment I decided to walk. I'd figured out street numbers and the avenues from tooling around with Desi and Mom, and it was a beautiful morning. At first, I was a little nervous about being completely on my own; ironic, since I'd walked across the bridge and through Desi's dangerous neighborhood all by myself the other night. But knowing my mom was in the same city, even if I would rather have died than been with her, had made me feel more secure. Now she was a thousand miles away.

But the more I walked, the better I felt. And everybody was so friendly—not at all the mean, rude types that some people in Wisconsin think New Yorkers are. "How ya' doin', sweetheart?" said a man spraying down the sidewalk in front of a grocery store. A cop smiled at me and put out his hand to help me down the curb. And at the bagel store, the guy laughed when I asked for extra butter.

Finally I arrived at the address Raquel had given me: 4 Times Square. I had to tilt my head all the way back to see to the top of the glass and steel building. Chic-looking women hurried around me and through the front doors as I stood and gawked. I was glad I'd walked because it helped cancel out the nervousness that suddenly washed over me.

Me, a model? For *Vogue* magazine? Who was anybody

kidding? My fury at my mother had driven me to the Awesome offices, had fueled my signing of the contract and my sending my mother home without me. But now that I was faced with the reality of actually having to do this job, I was scared witless.

I could turn. Go home. Run. Forget any of this ever happened. I doubted anyone from Awesome Models would trek to Wisconsin and drag me back.

But then I imagined showing up in Eagle River tonight admitting that I'd made a mistake, telling my mother and Tom that it was too scary, I'd chickened out. And that would be it, there wouldn't be another chance. It would be Eagle River forever, and even though just yesterday that was all I wanted out of life, now I couldn't say for sure I could embrace that kind of peace without wondering what-if.

My voice trembling, I gave my name to the security guard and looked around the lobby, trying to gather my nerve. That's when I saw them, the other women who were as young as me, as tall as me, as thin as me, even as plain yet unusual-looking as me. There were only two or three of them, but still: It was as if I had never known I was from another planet until I recognized these fellow members of my tribe. I had always thought I was just an oddly configured human, but now I saw I was a perfectly normal member of a different species.

This insight gave me a new injection of confidence that at least got me up the elevator to the twelfth floor and through the locked glass doors into the magazine's reception area, with its caramel wood walls and huge black logo, hushed and elegant as a Swiss bank—or at least as the Swiss bank I read about in a mystery novel once. There the editor's assistant greeted me and led me through narrow hallways, past jammed racks of clothing, and then into the fashion department, where the windows opened out onto a vista of the wild lights and colors of Times Square.

I'm at *Vogue*, I kept thinking, my fashion bible, most delightful companion through the long Wisconsin winters. Desi and I had our encyclopedic knowledge of *Vogue* in common: We discussed stories as if they were events in our lives. And now I was finally here, at the mother ship.

I expected thunder, I expected lightning, I expected at least dramatic music and fabulous clothes. But the *Vogue* offices were muted and neutral, something like the Motor Club offices where I went once with Mom. The desks were all squished together, there was gray industrial carpeting, and everybody was dressed like, well, kind of like Amish women, with higher-heeled shoes and without the hats. These women, with their makeupless faces and severe haircuts and their black and gray clothes, looked more like nuns than like the fashion editors in *The Devil Wears Prada*. When I was finally introduced to the trio of editors who were waiting to greet me, I couldn't help but blurt, "You all are so *plain!*"

I was relieved when they laughed at that instead of reporting me to Raquel for violating the models-should-be-seen-and-not-heard rule. Then they instantly grew somber again, as if preparing to discuss the real reason we were gathered here: The atom bomb, or the AIDS epidemic, or some other Serious Subject. The leader of the pack, who was very small and very thin, with large brown eyes and a worried-looking face, like a chihuahua, said, "We'd like to see how you look in some clothes. Let's go into the closet."

"The closet" turned out to be a room bigger than the entire House O' Pies, with mirrors along one long wall and cascades of jewelry and belts and scarves hung all up and down the other. Shoes were in a separate, smaller closet—though even the shoes lived in a room bigger than the bedroom I theoretically shared with Tatiana.

"We'll start with this," said the Chihuahua Woman, thrusting a pink silk Charmeuse bias-cut cocktail dress toward me.

"Oh my gosh," I said, afraid to touch it. "Is that an *Oscar?*"

The three women exchanged glances again, though considerably less amused ones than when I said they were plain.

"Very astute," said the blonde editor, who had a British accent. "You can change behind there."

She indicated a folding screen set up in the corner near the mirror.

"And please take everything else off," she said. Her accent made her sound like one of those teachers in the movies that even the baddest kids can't help but obey.

"You mean . . ." I said, afraid to go on because of what Raquel had said. But afraid not to go on, also.

"Yes," she said. "Even the thong."

Well, I wasn't wearing a thong, I was wearing my regular white cotton panties, but I knew what she meant. The air conditioning was on so high I had goose bumps all over my body, but I felt better once I zipped up the dress. The fabric was as thick and soft as Tom's best old chamois shirt, the one he gave me to sleep in. I stepped out from behind the screen and the triumvirate surveyed me from the neck down.

"The thighs could be a problem," said the third woman,

the non-British, non-chihuahua one, who was a bit pear-shaped herself.

"What do you mean—*jiggly?*" British accent said.

"No, not fat. Too thin."

"There's no such thing as thighs that are too thin," the leader cut in. "Besides, she's got very long calves. That's the key to everything."

Long calves were the key to everything? To love, happiness, and great personal wealth? I snorted.

All three of them went silent, staring in my direction as if I'd belched. Finally, the leader extended a silver sequined sheath to me. "Put this on," she said. I guess the Silent Rule included snorting.

I slipped the dress over my head and stepped out from behind the screen.

"This one is fabulous on her," said the leader woman, walking over to me and tugging at the dress's waist.

"Very Edie, very Andy," said Pear Shape. "Very Liza and Halston at Studio 54."

"She has fabulous tits," said the leader, though she apparently thought I didn't have ears.

Pear Shape nodded as I began to shiver. "We could put her in that black strapless," she said.

"We could do it like Stella," British said, "with long feather earrings and bare feet."

"Or like Marc," the leader said, "with those high black shoes and one of those caps."

"Or like my friend Desi!" I said excitedly, imagining how much Desi would love this dress, this whole place. "She'd probably go totally silver, with big mirrored earrings and shiny high-heeled sandals and something like those skinny silver Indian bangles all the way up both arms."

Finally they all looked at my face. The British woman and Pear Shape both opened their mouths, just a little, but enough to let me know they'd never heard anyone say this particular thing before and had no idea how to respond.

Leader Woman, on the other hand, pressed her lips tightly together. She looked like a narrow pipe that was building steam.

"No!" she finally exploded.

Everyone stood there, stunned for a moment.

"You're not here to offer your opinion, is that understood?" she said.

I hung my head. "Yes, ma'am."

"Don't call me ma'am—it makes me feel a hundred and twelve," she snapped. "Didn't Raquel go over the rules with you?"

Afraid to say anything at all, I mutely nodded.

They turned away from me then and began talking about locations, props, schedules. I slipped behind the screen and lifted the sequined dress over my head. I looked around for someplace to hang it, and finally let it drop onto the floor. When I had dressed and stepped back into the room, they were still talking, pulling jewelry from the accessory wall, beginning to lay out outfits on the floor the way I did when I was going out.

The only difference was that the outfits I laid out at home usually consisted of something like a huge shirt of Duke's over patent leather hot pants from the thrift store over my old dance class leggings, with red sneakers and a necklace

Tom had made me from pinecones, and the outfits they were laying out at *Vogue* were designed by Chanel and Marni with jewelry from Cartier and shoes from Louboutin. It was all I could do not to drool.

I put my hand on the doorknob, figuring this was my chance to make a silent getaway, when the Leader called out to me.

"You," she said. "Where do you think you're going?"

"Uh," I said, nervous about speaking but feeling as if I had no choice. "Out?"

"Not so fast," she said. "We're going to need you at nine o'clock tomorrow morning for the shoot. I'll phone Raquel with the details."

Now I really was speechless. If I'd understood her correctly, I was about to be in *Vogue* magazine.

Somehow I managed to keep my cool going down in the elevator and walking through the lobby. I even managed to push through the crowd in Times Square and head down into the subway station without grabbing any strangers and shouting my amazing news. But when a train roared into the station and I knew no one could hear me, I let myself scream at the top of my lungs from the sheer thrill of it.

Me, in *Vogue* magazine. If it hadn't been for the sound of the train, they might have heard me all the way in Wisconsin.

· · ·

The first person I saw when I walked into the loft where the *Vogue* shoot was taking place was Alex Pradels. That's right, Alex, the snobby photographer who'd taken my picture.

When he saw me, his face broke into a smile and he stood up.

"You owe me a big kiss," he said.

"Really?" The *nerve* of this man!

"I'm the one who got you this job," he continued, still maddeningly calm.

I frowned. "What are you talking about?"

"When your roommate Tatiana didn't show up for her fitting and they fired her, I recommended you."

"Wow," I said. "You did?"

"You are a star, my dear," he said, zooming in as if to kiss me.

I leaped back in alarm. "Thank you," I said, rubbing my cheek as if he'd slapped it rather than simply aimed his lips in its direction. "I better get to work."

"Work," for me at least, involved sitting around letting people fix me up. Now I know what a painter's canvas feels like, I thought, as my face was painted and powdered, as my hair was brushed and teased. It was like it had been for the test shots the other day times ten—more people, more time, more tension, more excitement.

We were shooting in a loft as big as Tom's uncle's hay barn, looking over the Hudson River and all of New York Harbor. I kept trying to breathe deeply while focusing on the Statue of Liberty in order to calm my nerves, but my brain kept ping-ponging off in crazy directions. The statue itself, for instance, made me think of France and my real father. Then that made me think of Mom and how far away she was. I'd try to turn my attention to the sailboats that dotted the harbor, but that only reminded me of Tom.

So instead of looking out the window I turned my attention to the loft. It was so beautiful, like no place I'd ever seen before, with all white furniture and huge paintings on the wall and enormous bouquets of white roses in shining glass globes. If you lived in this place, I imagined, you would never have an excuse to worry about anything, and imagining a life like that made me feel tranquil as everyone poked and prodded me and bustled around me.

Just when we were finally ready to shoot, the caterers arrived and set up lunch along the endless expanse of black countertop in the kitchen. There was more food than I'd seen anywhere outside the Fireman's Picnic—dishes unlike any I'd seen before coming to New York: plates of sushi as wide as the tires on Tom's truck, a mountain of vegetables as tall as Mom's Thanksgiving turkey, a salad like a pile of fall leaves just after raking, plus muffins and pies and cookies and candy that everybody ignored.

I imagined how much my mom would enjoy this spread, and then had to work to push her out of my mind so I didn't start feeling too sad. Now that I wasn't with her, I realized how often I thought about her, how many things—like, practically everything—reminded me of her.

Just think about what you're going to have for lunch, I counseled myself. But I suddenly felt self-conscious about eating with all these people standing around. Instead of filling my plate, I decided, I would only eat the one thing on the table I really wanted: the candy.

When I thought everyone was too busy with their sushi and their salad to notice, I slipped one of the dark chocolate balls from the pile and popped it in my mouth. But as I chewed, I saw that everyone was looking at me.

"These are really good," I said, figuring an explanation was called for.

They all kept staring until Yuki, Alex's assistant, finally reached out and took one of the chocolates, then lifted the sharp knife that was lying beside the bagels and sliced into the candy, popping a tiny wedge into her mouth.

Now it was my turn to stare. "I didn't know you could do that," I said finally.

"What?"

"Cut a piece of candy like a pie."

I noticed the others exchange glances.

"How long have you been working?" asked the hairdresser, a nice fellow who reminded me of my music teacher and dressed like him too.

I was so thrilled that someone had finally asked me a question that I wanted to give him a complete answer. "Oh, golly, I've been working as long as I can remember," I said, casting my mind back. "I was probably five when I started digging night crawlers for the bait shop."

Everyone took a step back, as if I had hit a fly ball.

"Amanda has recently arrived from the Midwest," Alex said.

"Ohhhhh," everyone said, as if he had explained that I'd recently been released from a mental hospital. I glared at him.

"You shouldn't be eating those chocolates if you're going to squeeze into the Charmeuse," said the British editor, who was the stylist—translation: person who got me dressed for the shoot.

"Now I'm going to have to redo her lipstick," said the makeup artist.

"You'll redo it twenty times anyway," Alex said, popping one of the chocolates into his own mouth. "Relax."

But British, whose name seemed to be Minty, was not to

be deterred. "Come along, Amanda," she said. "Let's get you dressed."

When the actual shoot started, an hour later, I stood teetering on heels so high I couldn't actually walk, with a fan blowing my hair back and lights making me squint and more than a dozen people standing in a semicircle staring at me. Alex took only a few shots before Minty called, "Stop!"

I blinked.

"She has to move," Minty said to Alex, loudly enough for me and everyone else to hear. "Will you please talk to her?"

He approached me. I stiffened. I mean, I stiffened more.

"Amanda," he said, leaning close. I swayed backward. He brought his lips to my ear. "She's got a stick up her behind, don't pay any attention to her," he mumbled.

In spite of myself, I smiled.

"Just do what you did the other day," he said.

"But it was only you and me then," I explained. "Plus, I didn't do anything."

"Wait here," he said.

He went over near where his equipment cases were stacked and fumbled around until he found what looked like a few sheets of paper, then returned to where I stood waiting.

"You probably haven't seen these," he said, handing them to me.

They were the contact sheets from the test shoot we'd done. I knew that was me in the photographs, but it was some far more beautiful, elegant, otherworldly version of me.

I looked at Alex, my eyes wide.

"How did you do this?"

He shrugged, that smile on his lips again. "How did *you* do it?"

"I don't know. I didn't do anything."

"That's exactly it: Don't do anything. But don't stand there waiting for me to take your picture either. Ignore everyone. Even ignore me. Just do what you want to do."

I knew what I wanted to do. Instead of going back into the spotlight, I headed to the food table. Minty started to protest but Alex shushed her. I got a chocolate. I came back to the light. Alex moved behind his camera. I stuck my tongue out and licked the chocolate.

"Great," Alex laughed, clicking. "That's beautiful."

"But the dress . . ." said Minty.

"Fuck the dress," said Alex. "You've got the most beautiful new girl in New York. Nobody gives a shit about the dress."

The most beautiful girl in New York? That made me want to laugh out loud, but not just because I thought it was ridiculous. I felt myself relax, and then the longer we worked, the more relaxed I grew, the happier Alex got, and the quieter everybody else became. I still didn't completely *like* him, but having him take my picture reminded me of going to the special dentist in Milwaukee who'd made me a new front tooth after I fell off my bike. I didn't exactly like the dentist either, but I trusted that he was good at his job and that he would be able to take care of me. That's the way I felt with Alex.

Things I Thought About While Alex Was Taking My Picture

1. How I was making enough money on this one day to take a trip to Europe, which I thought I would never be able to afford to do in my entire life.

2. Desi, and how great it would be, for both of us, if she were here.

3. How the silver sequined dress felt like chain mail on my body.

4. The princess in one of my favorite movies when I was a kid, *The Princess Bride*. (Fantasy inspired by the dress. Fantasy also inspired by the chain mail fantasy.)

5. Ice skating on Big Secret Lake with Tom. (This was when the air conditioner was turned up especially high and I started twirling to get warm.)

6. The pizza I'd eaten for dinner last night.

7. The other appointments Raquel had lined up for me this week.

8. Lipstick: how much I hated it.

9. Chocolate: how much I loved it.

10. Tatiana, who'd slept in her bed when I was out yesterday, refilled the apartment with cigarette smoke, and disappeared again before I got home.

By the end of the shoot, when everybody started packing up, relieved and happy because it had gone well and because it was over, I finally let go, really let go. I scrubbed all the makeup off and ran my hair under the faucet to rinse out all the spray. Then I realized I was finally and truly hungry, not just candy hungry, but buffalo burger ravenous. Forget sushi, salad, and vegetables; I piled my plate with roast beef with mayonnaise slathered on it, and helped myself to one of the beers in the refrigerator.

Alex sat down at the kitchen counter beside me as I wolfed down my food.

"Did you have fun?" he asked.

I shrugged. "A little." Then I let out the last of the breath I'd been holding in all day and finally smiled at him, for the very first time. "Thanks for helping me."

"My pleasure," he said. "I really like working with you. And I—well, I remember what it was like being new in New York."

"You do?"

"Of course. With this accent, you can tell I haven't been here forever, can't you? Listen, do you want to take some of this food home? It's going to take ages for you to get your check from this shoot, and I know Raquel's kind of stingy with the allowance she gives you girls."

"Wow," I said, "that would be great."

"And there's some other stuff we could grab too. Stockings, eye shadows, samples the editors always leave behind."

It was like Christmas at the Rotary Club. Somewhere in the middle of packing up the fifth container of food, Alex looked at me and said, "Are you sure you and Tatiana can eat all this?"

"Oh, it's not all for us," I said. As Alex and I packed the food I'd been hatching a plan. "I'm going to take everything down to my friend Desi's building on the Lower East Side and hand it out to the people who live there."

Alex looked at me, surprised. "Well," he said, packing faster, "that sounds like a very nice idea."

When everything was together, he helped me carry it downstairs, where he hailed me a taxi.

"So," he said, when I was about to step into the cab. "Would you like to have dinner with me sometime?"

I was about to say no because I was so used to disliking him. Then I was about to say no because of Tom.

As if reading my thoughts, he interrupted the silence to say, "Come on, I mean as friends. I feel a little bit responsible for you being here on your own. I'll take you someplace *magnifique*."

Who could resist *magnifique*, or a new friend, especially one who'd proven he had such friendly intentions?

"All right," I said.

"Saturday night?"

I nodded my agreement, but I was thinking about the plans I'd already made with Desi for Saturday, and scheming how I could keep one date without breaking the other.

five

So all this stuff was just free?" Desi said, as we knocked on another door in her tenement building.

"Yeah," I said, shaking my head. "They were going to throw it out."

"Who is it?" came a suspicious voice from behind the door.

"Mrs. Alvarez, it's me, Desi, from five. I have some free stuff for you."

"What is it?" Mrs. Alvarez said.

"It's food, Mrs. A. And treats. No tricks, I promise."

The door cracked open and a thin woman, a baby on her hip and a toddler clinging to her leg, peered out.

"My friend here got this food for free and we're giving it out to people in the building."

"Is it spoiled?"

"No, Mrs. A, it's totally good. Look, we got cakes, we got breads, milk, all these vegetables."

"I'll take some milk."

"Okay, take something else too. Take this cake. Some muffins."

"I don't need too much."

"Just take it."

When we moved on down the hall, Desi grinned at me and said, "I feel like Robin Freaking Hoodette."

I laughed. "It feels great to do something that actually helps somebody after how I spent my day."

I couldn't deny it: I loved luxurious clothes and expensive shoes and high fashion for its own sake. But I also knew how many essential things that much money could buy for people who had nothing.

"Hey," said Desi. "The world needs beauty too."

She knocked on the next door and handed an elderly neighbor a wedge of Brie, a bag of fruit, and several pieces of chocolate.

"You'd never believe it," I told her, "but it was that French photographer who took my test shots who suggested I take all this food and everything."

"He's got a thing for you," Desi said, heading up the stairs to her own apartment. "I know it."

"Noooooo," I said, but feeling myself blush. "Besides, it doesn't matter, because I'm not interested in him or anybody else. I love Tom."

"Tom's at the freaking North Pole. And you're here at the center of the universe."

"That doesn't change the way I feel about him," I said, taking the few remaining goodies from her so she could unlock her door. "Which reminds me: Want to go out to dinner Saturday after we hang out?"

"Sure," said Desi. "Where should we go?"

"Alex is taking us somewhere great."

"Alex is taking *us* out to dinner?"

"He invited me," I admitted, "but I need you to come along with us. So he doesn't get the wrong idea."

The door to Desi's apartment was open now, the usual family party in full swing inside. "I'm your friend," Desi said, "not your security guard."

"Please, Desi."

"Are you sure he isn't gay? I thought all guys in the fashion business were gay."

I'd never met a gay man, not that I knew of anyway. But if Alex Pradels was gay, why did I get such a funny feeling when I was with him?

"Come on, Desi. What are best friends for?"

She brightened. "I'm your best friend?"

"Of course!"

"In that case," she said, "I'll be there. Want to come in and kick it for a while?"

"Not tonight," I told her. "I've got to go home and crash."

. . .

I was fast asleep, dreaming that I was giving pies away to people on a ship, when I felt someone shaking my shoulder, hard. Thinking it was my mom waking me up for school, anticipating her soft voice and a gentle kiss on the cheek, I mumbled and rolled over.

"Wake up, new girl," said an accented voice. "I need you to come out with me."

"Huh?" I said sleepily, blinking up at a face that I slowly recognized as Tatiana's.

It was the first time I'd seen her since Raquel had introduced us, and I was having trouble piecing together what was going on, even after she switched on the bedroom lamp. She was dressed in the tiniest of denim work shirts—OshKosh B'Gosh children's wear, perhaps—with the sleeves hacked off, over a short white skirt with big iridescent sequins shimmering on it. On her feet were bright yellow high-heeled slides of the type worn by Barbie. Her copious honey-colored hair was piled high on her head, and her mascara was smudged—although on her it looked so good I could imagine thousands of fourteen-year-olds copying the look the next day.

"Let's go out," she repeated. "We make party."

Blearily I consulted the clock on the narrow table wedged between our two narrow beds.

"It's after midnight!" I said with alarm. "I thought you were coming home."

"Am coming home," she said. "But now going out again. Come on." She tugged on my arm, lifting me from the bed. "Come on, lazy girl."

"But Raquel said . . ."

Tatiana laughed. "Raquel is old lady. We are hot babes. Come."

"I don't have anything to wear," I said. At least not anything like a tighter-than-skin denim shirt and the sequined headband Tatiana was wearing as a skirt.

"Yes you have," Tatiana said gravely. "Today, I test-drive all your clothes."

I thought everything looked distinctly messier than it had when I put it away. She opened the top drawer of my dresser and without hesitation pulled out one of Desi's creations, the short dress made from vintage material she'd been working on the night I stayed at her house.

"This," she said, "is butchin'."

I figured she meant bitchin', but I didn't really think it would be any better if she said it right.

"My friend Desi designed that."

"Desi is genius," Tatiana pronounced. "Wear this, I style you."

Instead of a jewelry box, Tatiana had a tool kit as big as the ones guys hauled in the back of their pickups. It was so heavy she actually couldn't lift it, but had to slide it out from the floor of her closet, where it had been buried under a heap of dirty clothes and jumbled shoes. Her idea of "butchin'" accessories were gold hoops so big they rested on my shoulders and sandals so high I couldn't stand in them, never mind walk.

"The earrings are cool," I told her. "But I'm sorry, Tatiana. I can't handle these shoes."

"Call me Tati," she said. "And you *will* handle shoes. You are supermodel now."

My first day out, and I'd already been promoted from model to supermodel.

Downstairs, I was stunned to find an enormous stretch limo, as shiny as my black patent leather confirmation shoes, idling at the curb in wait for us.

"Did Raquel send this?" I asked, my eyes widening.

"Raquel, ha! This is boyfriend's car. Or maybe—" she said, darkening, "ex-boyfriend's."

From the looks of it, a party had already been in progress in the back of the limo. Just like our apartment, it too was filled with smoke, and it too had discarded champagne bottles on the floor. Once we were inside, Tati didn't have to say a word and the car glided purposefully into the traffic.

"Where are we going?" I asked her.

"Hot club," she said, popping the cork on a fresh bottle of champagne and pouring me a crystal glass full. "We're hunting."

"What are we hunting for?"

"For *boyfriend*"—that word seemed to automatically cause her brows to knit and her mouth to turn down—"of course."

I was nervous that Raquel would call to check up on us in the middle of the night, or that maybe the agency had security cameras installed in our apartment, but then I told myself no, that was impossible. As long as we got up on time, as long as we showed up for our go-sees and our bookings, we wouldn't get in trouble. Heck, Tati didn't even seem to do that and Raquel hadn't put her on a plane back to Ukraine.

The car glided to a stop in front of a dark building, marked only with a large gold number 13, where there was a crowd of people congregated on the sidewalk. Without waiting for the driver to open the door, Tati pulled me out of the car, champagne glass still in hand, and toward the building's door. The crowd parted for us as if we were radioactive. A flash went off.

"Look cool," Tati ordered.

I had no idea how to do that, especially not with these torture devices strapped to my feet, so I decided that as long as I didn't visibly sweat or say "Golly" too often, I'd be okay.

Barely pausing, Tati kissed the cheek of the extremely large man guarding the door. "Hello, Rocco," she said, gesturing to me. "This is Amanda, new girl."

Rocco nodded to me and held the door open, slamming it shut behind us.

Inside, it took a few moments for my eyes to adjust to the darkness. Tiny candles flickered everywhere. Everyone, it seemed, was thin. Everyone was young. Everyone and everything was cool.

"We dance," Tati said, taking my hand.

Wasn't that uncool, dancing with your girlfriend? At Northland Pines, it would get you talked about big-time in the halls the next day. But there was not necessarily a lot of crossover, I was learning, between what was cool at high school in Eagle River and what was cool in Manhattan.

Things That Are Cooler in Eagle River Than in Manhattan

1. Having a neck that sticks out wider than your head.
2. Having tires that stick out wider than your car.
3. Drinking beer till you pass out.
4. Snowmobiling.

5. Wearing a cheese head, drinking milk, tipping cows—basically anything related to cattle or dairy products.

6. Skinny-dipping, wearing shorts in winter, going barefoot—though I couldn't extend that to include every kind of nakedness, judging from the amount of bare skin around me in the club.

7. Lip gloss.

8. Blow-drying your hair so that it looks like you blow-dried it.

9. Having a baby and thinking up a name for it that all your friends think is cute but that's spelled differently than anyone's ever spelled it before, like Ryeleigh.

Things That Are Cooler in Manhattan Than in Eagle River

1. Spending a lot of money on a haircut that looks like you chopped it off yourself with an ax. And without a mirror.

2. Black clothing. Black anything.

3. The word "actually."

4. Saying you'd love to have a baby but then never actually getting pregnant.

5. Therapy.

6. Being alone.

7. Being gay.

8. Being French.

9. Vegetables.

Tatiana leaned close to me. "Oh, good," she said into my ear. "Boyfriend is here. Dance closer."

She shimmied toward me and bumped her hip against mine, putting her hands above her head and rotating her pelvis like one of those girls who dance in cages. Somebody in the crowd whistled, and Tati ripped open all but one of the snaps on her denim shirt. My own dancing was hobbled by my high shoes, but that didn't seem to matter to Tati or the enthusiasm of what had turned into our audience. People were clapping and more and more flashes were going off.

Suddenly a man in a gray suit pushed between us, facing Tati. He looked wealthy, conservative, like a businessman, but he was gorgeous too, dark and muscular, somehow managing to make his gray suit and white shirt look sexy. And the even more remarkable thing was that he also looked nice, his handsome face sincere, his gaze focused adoringly on Tatiana.

Tatiana kept dancing, her eyes cast down, but he spoke urgently into her ear. She continued to pretend to ignore him, but I could tell she was listening. I continued to dance, but only so I could stay close enough to hear them.

"Goddamn it, Tati, I love you, you know that," the man said.

Tatiana turned determinedly away from him, dancing in a circle so that she was facing in the other direction. I wiggled over so I was facing her, and was astonished to see that she was blinking back tears.

"Are you okay?" I asked her.

"He don't care," she said.

I turned to Mr. Billings (that turned out to be his name), who looked at me mournfully with his big chocolate brown eyes.

"She doesn't think you care."

"Please tell her that I love her," he said into my ear.

I danced back to Tati. "He says he loves you."

"Tell him I don't believe him," she said back.

"She doesn't believe you."

He rolled his eyes and practically groaned in desperation. "Ask her what I have to do to persuade her."

"He wants to know . . ."

"Tell him to go freak off!"

Well, I wasn't going to tell him that, so I just smiled and shrugged, and he smiled and shrugged back at me. He was so suave-looking, except he had a little snaggle tooth, which to my mind was the thing that made him really irresistible. He seemed like a great guy to me, and I couldn't understand Tatiana's problem with him, though he didn't seem any more enlightened than I was.

After a moment's hesitation, he moved close to Tati and put his hands on her hips. When she didn't swat them away, he moved closer to her and started dancing in rhythm to her. He was a really great dancer, almost as good as Tati herself. She began dancing away from me, her boyfriend holding tight to her tail, both moving farther and farther from me, like a train chugging west.

Another man, with red hair sticking out all over his head and thick-rimmed black glasses, took advantage of the gap and danced up to me. The odd thing was that he was carrying a notebook and a Bic pen that was leaking onto his fingers.

"Hello, beautiful," he said. "You must be a new girl. What's your name?"

"Amanda," I said.

He wrote that down, without asking my last name.

"And what agency are you with?"

"How do you know I'm a model?" I asked.

He laughed, ignoring my question and instead asking, "Whose clothes are you wearing tonight?"

I stopped dancing and looked down at the dress Desi had made me. "Why," I said, "my own."

"Charming!" he cried, scribbling another note on his pad as a flash went off so close to my eyes I was temporarily blinded.

By the time I could see clearly again, the red-haired man had disappeared and so had Tati and her boyfriend. I pushed my way through the room as quickly as I could manage on the ridiculous heels, but they were nowhere to be found. It hadn't even occurred to me to bring money along; I was with Tati, she would get me home. Someone tried to hand me a glass of champagne and another man asked me to dance, but I sat at the bar to get off my feet, hoping that Tatiana would once again appear, wishing with sudden longing that Tom were there. It almost made me laugh out loud to imagine Tom in a place like this, but I loved thinking of his strong arms lifting me clear into the air, carrying me outside and home—Wisconsin home or Manhattan home, it didn't matter—safe with him.

Finally I gave up waiting for Tom or any other White Knight to come along and save me, and fought my way outside, where at least I could get a cell signal to call Desi or start trying to stagger in my heels toward home. But when I reached the sidewalk in front of the club, I was surprised to find the chauffeur waiting for me.

"Miss Tati asked that I drive you home," he said.

"Where did she go?"

"She went with Mr. Billings to his town house."

"Oh," I said. "All right. I'll go home."

. . .

Since I hadn't spent any time with Tati in the apartment, I hadn't missed her being there before, but when I got back that night I did. For the first time since I'd been in New York, I felt lonely, really and truly lonely.

Feeling like this, the first person I thought of was my mom. If I wanted to talk before bed, or if I woke up in the middle of the night and couldn't get back to sleep, Mom had always been there.

But I didn't want Mom to be the one who was there for me now. I was an adult, I reminded myself, I'd made my break. I couldn't go running to Mommy.

Tom. In the summer, Tom was always in bed by nine so he could be up before dawn to take one client or another fishing. But more than once I'd called him or sneaked into his room in the middle of the night. He wouldn't mind.

At the first sound of his muffled sleepy voice, I nearly melted. It sounded as if he were right there in the bed next to me. That combined with the memory of Tati dancing with her boyfriend made me long to feel Tom's arms around me, tight as they had been in the airport.

"Oh, Tommy," I groaned, falling back onto my pillow. "I miss you so bad."

"Me too, baby," he said huskily.

"Can't you come here, Tommy? Come to New York and visit me."

He was silent for a long minute, and then he said, "Nope."

"Oh, come on, Tom. It would be so much fun. I have an apartment where we could stay. I even have enough money to buy you a plane ticket."

"I have work," he said.

"So, some old rich guy doesn't catch a trout. I really need to see you, Tommy."

"Come here," he said.

Now I was the one who went silent. If I could afford to buy him a ticket to visit me, I could afford to buy myself one to go back home. I didn't have any work scheduled for this weekend; all I had to do was blow off Alex and Desi. I could fly home and back so quickly no one would ever have to know I was even gone.

But I would know. And Tom would know, even if he didn't tell my mom and Duke. That would be weird, trying to sneak around in a town where every single person knew me. Plus, the real point was that I wanted Tom to come here, so I could show him the place where I had my new life. And maybe if Tom were with me, I'd learn to feel more at home here.

"I really want to take you around New York so when we talk you'll know what I'm talking about," I tried to explain. "We could go to Chinatown, to the top of the Empire State Building, the Statue of Liberty . . ."

He interrupted me. "Can't do it, Amanda."

I hesitated. "Why not?"

"Work," he said. "Money."

"But I already told you," I began, "I have enough money and it wouldn't have to be for long . . ."

He interrupted me with a single word: "Can't."

I knew what that meant, in Wisconsinese. It meant "won't." It meant "don't want to." Except wanting or not wanting to wasn't considered a good enough reason for anything in Wisconsin.

I felt slapped. I knew that pressing him wasn't going to get me any more information or help me understand what was happening to us. Even if I were with him now, he probably wouldn't tell me exactly why he couldn't or wouldn't come to New York to visit me. Maybe he didn't even understand it himself.

That made me realize not only how far apart we were, but that the distance was growing. Instead of feeling like he was right next to me on the pillow, or even a thousand miles away, it felt as if we lived on distant planets, with not even our language in common.

"We were going to get married, Tom," I said.

He interrupted me. "Were?"

That shook me. I felt my arms begin to tremble as my breath grew jagged.

"Yes, *were*," I said. I was trying to keep my voice calm—Tom hated yelling—but I wasn't succeeding. My volume began to rise as I felt myself grow more upset. "I was willing to live *your* life, Tom—fishing and hunting and camping and staying in Eagle River forever. So now that I have something of my own, why *can't* you share my new world?"

"That's just not me, Amanda," Tom said, his voice still maddeningly level. "If you want some guy to carry your fancy shopping bags and put a tie on to go to a chichi New York restaurant, you're going to have to find somebody else."

"Maybe I will!" I screamed. "Maybe I'll find somebody

who doesn't smell like worms and has been someplace more interesting than *Milwaukee!*"

Then I think I actually growled, and I slammed down the phone. I felt a moment of satisfaction—I showed him!—until I realized I was now more alone than ever.

six

So you broke up?"

Desi and I were in the Kiehl's Pharmacy on Third Avenue, one of the oldest shops in Manhattan, moving methodically down the aisles rubbing tester creams and lotions into our skin. Desi at least was sniffing before she rubbed, while I was slathering on every single thing I came to without thinking.

"We didn't break up, exactly," I said. "But we had a huge fight."

"Did anybody threaten to crucify anybody?" Desi asked, dabbing moisturizer from a sea blue jar on her forehead.

I conceded crucifixion had not been threatened.

"Were any weapons mentioned or produced?"

No, I said, no weapons.

Desi shrugged. "Well, where I come from, that's not a serious fight."

"You don't understand," I said. "We've never even raised our voices before."

"Then maybe you were overdue."

I didn't know about that, but I knew things were changing between me and Tom. It had been naïve of me to think I could make such a major shift and our relationship would stay exactly the same. Even if Tom refused to change, *we* couldn't help changing. But I wasn't sure what that meant.

It was Saturday morning, and Desi and I had met up early so she could take me on a tour of the New York I hadn't already seen. When Mom was here we'd visited all the big tourist attractions and shopped at Bloomingdale's and Barneys and H & M. We'd eaten corned beef at the Stage Deli and had tea at The Pierre and gone to a Broadway show. And of course Desi and I had already done SoHo and Canal Street and the East Village.

Today, she said, she was going to show me some of her favorite places in New York that most people only got to when they lived here—and a lot of them not even then. We'd started the day with coffee at Caffe Reggio in the Village, and then we walked over to Kiehl's. Now we each bought a tiny bottle of shower gel—mango for Desi, grapefruit for me—and headed back outside and downtown toward the Dumpling Man on St. Mark's Place, where Desi promised me they had more different kinds of dumplings than Mom had pies.

"I don't understand how Tom could not want to see all

this," I said to Desi, gesturing toward the busy avenue and the parade of outrageously dressed people. "I mean, maybe he wouldn't be into SoHo, but I know he'd love Central Park, even something like the Statue of Liberty."

"Maybe he's afraid," Desi said.

I was so accustomed to thinking of Tom as strong and fearless and brave that this possibility hadn't occurred to me.

"What makes you think that?" I asked Desi.

She shrugged. "I get afraid," she said. "Like, I'm afraid to go anyplace besides New York."

"Well, I'd be afraid to go to Europe or Asia or something too," I assured her. "But if you're staying in America . . ."

"No, that's not what I mean. I mean I'd be afraid to go to Wisconsin." She laughed a little. "Hell, I'm afraid to go to New Jersey. I've never been anywhere but here, Amanda."

"You mean . . ."

"I've never been out of New York City. Okay, I've been to Staten Island on the ferry, over to Brooklyn, to the New York Botanical Garden in the Bronx on a class trip once, but those are still technically New York. California, Jersey, even Long Island—fuhgeddaboutit."

This was as astounding to me as Tom not wanting to visit me in New York, until I remembered that up to a few weeks ago, I'd never been out of Wisconsin.

"But you want to go other places," I said to Desi, remembering how excited I'd been about my trip to New York. "You'd love northern Wisconsin. I'd love to take you there."

"I don't know," she said. "For a long time I never went anyplace because we didn't have any money and I didn't know anybody who lived anywhere but here. But now"—

she shrugged again—"the thought of being someplace strange like that makes my hands sweat and my stomach go all queasy just thinking about it. I don't know if I want to go anyplace else."

I was about to argue with her but then I thought, This is not something I'm going to be able to talk her out of. She might have hit on something about Tom. Tom might be scared of coming to New York, or he might just have made up his mind that he'd hate it here so there was no point in coming. And maybe, I had to admit to myself, he was even right. I loved it so I wanted him to love it, yet the truth was I had never seen any evidence that he would.

But Desi—Desi had an adventurous soul. She had the drive to break out of the limitations she was born into. I could *imagine* her in Paris or Tokyo even more easily than I could imagine myself, could see her loving it there. Someday, I thought, I'll just buy her a ticket and get her onto a plane and the rest will take care of itself.

Today, though, she was my guide. We rode the subway all the way out to Coney Island, where I saw the ocean for the first time, though Desi was more interested in the kitschy attractions of the boardwalk. Then we went to Central Park and rowed a boat on the lake. It was funny to me that Desi thought the most amazing things about New York were the ones they had all over the place in Eagle River. And then we meandered through the park to meet Alex for dinner.

We found the Time Warner Center and made our way to the J.Crew store, where Alex was waiting near the candy-colored cotton sweaters. He smiled when he saw me and kissed my cheek, but looked surprised when he saw Desi.

"This is my girlfriend, Desi," I told him.

"Oh," he said, shaking her hand. "*Enchanté.*"

"I asked Desi to come to dinner with us," I said.

He raised his eyebrows, but quickly nodded. "I understand. That's totally fine."

"But if you don't want me here . . ." Desi began.

I kicked her ankle. "No, it's fine, isn't it, Alex?"

"Of course," he said smoothly. "I'm sure the restaurant will be happy to accommodate another guest."

He led us onto the escalator, heading up rather than down, as I'd expected.

"Where are we going?" I asked suspiciously, thinking he might be trying to lure us to some private apartment.

"You'll see," he said, a twinkle in his eye.

"No fucking way," said Desi.

"What?" I asked, my heart seizing up.

"You're not," she said to Alex.

"Not what?" he asked, in a teasing voice.

We were on the fourth floor, and he was leading us past an elegant grouping of velvet and leather chairs and sofas, much more elegant than I'd seen in any mall, even the one in Wauwatosa.

Desi stopped still. "I can't. Amanda, I know I said I'd come with you, but I can't let someone who doesn't even know me treat me to a dinner like this."

"What are you talking about?" I wailed in frustration.

"He's taking you to Per Se," Desi explained. "That's one of the best restaurants in New York—in the world. And one of the most expensive."

I looked questioningly toward Alex, but he refused to meet my eye.

"I'm taking *both* of you," he said, lightly touching Desi's back and urging her forward. "Please. I insist."

The entrance to Per Se seemed to be through two tall doors painted an elegant shade of dark blue, but when we approached the doors a thick glass panel to one side mysteriously slid open, like something in a James Bond movie. Inside, all was dim, serene, plush, and modern, with wood paneling and steel accents and a wall of glass looking down over the darkening park where Desi and I had just been walking.

Suddenly I felt self-conscious about what I was wearing, a short ruffly skirt from vintage material that Desi had made and a black tank top and flip-flops onto which Desi had glued big red plastic roses. Desi was dressed in her usual body-camouflaging black, as severe and chic as any *Vogue* editor.

"I'm not dressed right," I whispered in panic to Alex.

"You look *magnifique*," he assured me.

He was wearing loose white pants and a white tee shirt and a navy blue linen jacket over that. On his feet, I was cheered to see, were flip-flops.

"I'm proud to be with you both," he said.

The restaurant wasn't very big, but the tables were as roomy and spread as far apart as they were at the fanciest supper club in northern Wisconsin. It had the same luxurious feeling as the park it overlooked: that sense of space. I felt myself relax into the emptiness, felt myself grow more confident as the waiters and waitresses, totally professional yet sweet and down-to-earth, asked me what I wanted and ferried amazing food and drinks to our table as we gazed out on the fairy-tale lights of the city.

Just about every single thing I ate and drank was something I'd never had to eat or drink before. I didn't feel like lying about my age and getting Alex into trouble, so the wine guy suggested "the nonalcoholic beverage pairing," pouring Desi and me a procession of sparkling ciders and fruity sodas and iced tea made with leaves gathered by mountain goats high in the Himalayas, or something like that.

We didn't get to pick our own food and I was a little worried that I might not like it, but I ended up scraping up every tiny scrap from every dish they set before me, trying to memorize each detail so that when I was finally talking to Mom again, I'd be able to tell her all about it. Here's what we had:

- Oysters and caviar.
- Foie gras, which tasted even better than my grandpa Trippel's liver sausage.
- Grilled pompano from Florida, good enough to put any Wisconsin Friday night fish fry to shame.
- Lobster in a sauce so sweet that Desi and I insisted it must be made from sugar, though Alex assured us it was not.
- Something they called "barbeque" that Desi kept marveling was better than what her neighbor Mrs. Alvarez made.
- Prime rib that was delicious, though it was hard to enjoy it because that's Mom's favorite, so it made me want to tell Mom all about this dinner, though I still was convinced that I was not going to call her.
- A salad whose leaves were the exact color of Alex's eyes.
- Grapefruit sorbet that didn't remind me of anything except grapefruit, thank goodness.
- A caramel and hot fudge sundae that just might have been better than the one at JoAnn's Dairy Bar.

- Lots of little cookies and chocolates, as if we were still hungry—but we ate them anyway!

By the time we left, it was nearly eleven and we all felt relaxed and happy, putting our arms around each other and strolling down Broadway as if it were the middle of a Sunday afternoon. Finally Alex hailed a cab and directed it downtown.

"Where are we going?" I asked.

"Bar 13," he said—that place Tati had taken me the other night.

Desi settled back happily into the taxi. "I've always wanted to go there," she said, smiling. "Thank you, Alex. And thank *you*, Amanda, for inviting me along tonight."

She took my hand and held on to it, and I thought of what she'd told me, about how she'd never gone anywhere. I was grateful to Alex for doing something to change that, even if we were still in New York. I may not have been dying to go back to Bar 13 and subject myself to that level of cool again so soon, but if Desi wanted the experience, it was all good with me.

When we pulled up to the club, there was an even larger crowd on the sidewalk than there had been the night before. Just as Tati had, Alex walked confidently through the crowd, greeting Rocco, who magically opened the door.

"Hi, Rocco," I said, waving to him. He smiled in recognition and silently admitted me.

But I had just stepped over the threshold when I heard the door bang closed behind me. I swiveled around, but Desi wasn't there.

I had to hammer on the door to get Rocco to open it back up again. Immediately I spotted Desi standing against the ropes, looking horrified.

"She's with us," I explained to Rocco, certain that it had been a misunderstanding, that Desi would automatically be allowed in.

But Rocco kept staring straight ahead.

Now Alex was by my side, taking in what was going on.

"Rocco," he said. "There are three in my party."

Rocco stood fast.

Looking confused, Alex took a bill—I saw it was a hundred—out of his wallet and waved it toward Rocco. "I said the girl is with us."

Rocco crossed his substantial arms over his chest. "Sorry. Full," he finally said.

"It's all right," said Desi, shooting Rocco a dirty look. "I'm tired anyway."

"No!" I said. I turned to Rocco. "Come on. This is crazy. You know me. I was here with Tatiana last night. You know, Tatiana, the model."

"You're in," Rocco said.

"You go ahead," Desi said. "It was supposed to be just you and Alex anyway."

"No," I said, furious, turning on Rocco. "Why am I in and my friend isn't? Because I'm taller? Thinner? Because her skin is darker?"

Now that I was paying attention, it was clear that everyone who was being let into the club was cut from the same mold, like Stepford Partyers: They were all tall, thin, beautiful, smooth, chic in the most obvious way, like they could have stepped from an ad in a magazine. Desi certainly didn't fit that glossy profile, and Rocco steadfastly ignored her, mimicking one of those statues on Easter Island, stony, immovable.

"Never mind," said Alex, putting the money back in his pocket. "This place has a bad smell anyway."

"I'm going to tell Tatiana and Mr. Billings how incredibly rude this place is," I said, taking Desi's arm, gratified that I at last seemed to have shaken the statue.

But it was too late, we were on our way, me and Alex flanking Desi, arms linked through hers. We kept walking, none of us talking, for a long time, until finally Alex suggested we go into a quiet-looking bar we were passing and just relax for a while, try to end the evening on an up note.

"Nah," Desi said. "I'm so tired. I just want to go home."

Neither of us could blame her, so we didn't try to argue. We kept walking until we had delivered Desi safely to her door, and then we turned around and started hiking back toward my place.

"I'm sorry about that," Alex said finally.

"It wasn't your fault."

"Maybe not. But if you go to that kind of place, you should be aware of what it feels like to be on the wrong side of the ropes."

"I've always been on the wrong side of the ropes," I told him.

He gave a short, sharp laugh, but then he saw that I was serious.

"You?" he said. "How can that be?"

"I was always different," I said. "Where I come from, 'different' is what people call something that's ugly or weird or frightening when they don't want to come right out and say how much they don't like it."

"Yes," he said gently. "But you were different because you were beautiful. Surely that is not a bad thing?"

I shook my head. "Beautiful is not how I felt," I told him. "Just tall and skinny and strange-looking. But it wasn't just my looks that made me different."

"Ah," he said. "I understand."

"You do?" I said.

"You perhaps had . . . different interests from the other girls."

"I did," I said decisively, surprised that he knew this. "I mean, I liked to fish and hunt and camp, and not a lot of girls liked doing those things. But then I also liked clothes and fashion. I was dying to come to New York, even just to go to the little college in a bigger town. It got so that by the end of high school, I had to go online to find people I could connect with, people who were like me."

"Like Desi," Alex said gently.

"Yes, like Desi."

Walking with Alex, listening to his accent, made me think about the other way I felt different, the thing I hadn't been conscious of until this trip but that perhaps, down deep, I'd known about all along.

"There's something else," I told Alex, "something my mom told me that night when you first took my picture. I grew up thinking that my mother's husband, who is this really nice Wisconsin guy, was my father. But the truth is my real father is French. He's a photographer." I laughed a little. "Just like you."

"But maybe," Alex said, "that is not such a terrible thing. I would take you for a French girl, with that black hair and those skinny hips. Who is this photographer father of yours?"

"I don't know much about him, where he is, whether he's even still alive. My mother never kept in touch with him, never even told him she was pregnant. All I know is that his name is Jean-Pierre Renaud . . ."

"Wait a minute," Alex said, and stopped walking. "*The* Jean-Pierre Renaud?"

"I don't know," I said, confused. "Maybe."

"There's a fashion photographer named Jean-Pierre Renaud who's very well known in Europe. He worked in New York for a while—I don't know, twenty, twenty-five years ago, but since then he's been based in Paris, working for French *Vogue,* Italian *Vogue,* that kind of thing." Alex was looking at me strangely.

"That might be him," I said. "What do you know about him?"

"Not much," said Alex, "though his work, *j'adore.* I met him once, very briefly, when I was just starting out. I interviewed to be his assistant. I didn't get the job."

"What was he like?"

"You know, it was an odd situation, because I was the beginner, the young boy, and he was the great man. This was maybe ten years ago, and at that time he was in his forties. So older than your mom, I think. But now that I remember it . . ."

He was still staring at me, and began nodding his head.

"Yes, yes," he said, "There's definitely a resemblance. He's very tall and thin, with black hair and intense dark eyes. He had this eccentric laugh and this unique style. Like, well . . ."

"Like what?"

He hesitated for a moment. "Like you," he said.

It was one thing to discover that my real father was somewhere out there, a theoretical man who could be anywhere, doing anything, who I might never be able to find even if I wanted to, who might not even be alive. It was another to discover that I was walking down the street with someone who'd actually met him. Who could probably, with a phone call or two, put me in touch with him tomorrow.

"Really?" I asked, feeling my heart beat faster, overwhelmed at the idea that this person who held the genetic key to my identity had suddenly moved so much closer to being real. All I had to do was reach out and I could touch him, talk to him, discover a whole new dimension of myself. "Do you know how I could find him? Do you have his address? Or maybe his phone number?"

"I might have saved it," he said. "Or I seem to remember an editor I know in Paris, Danique, once had a little thing with him. She probably knows . . ."

"No no no!" I chanted, stopping dead still and sticking my fingers in my ears.

I shocked even myself by how childishly I was acting. But the closer my father got to being a living, breathing man, a man with *girlfriends,* the more I felt myself freak out.

"It's all right," said Alex, touching my arm. "I thought you were saying you wanted to get in touch with him."

"I do!" I said. "Or no, I don't! Oh God, I don't know. I don't know what I want. It's all too much, too fast."

"It's okay," he said, gently taking my arm and leading me

forward. "You have time. You don't have to decide anything now."

He had a way of helping me calm down. As we walked, I began to breathe more deeply, to feel myself reinhabiting my own body. And as I began to be aware of my own body again, I started to notice *his.* He was about my height, not nearly as tall as Tom, but that was nice: I could look directly into his eyes. He wasn't as muscular as Tom either, but he was slim and graceful, his arm hard through the fabric of his shirt. I found myself thinking about his fingers, imagining how long they must be, and agile, on account of all that fiddling with the camera.

I shook my head briskly, to try to clear it of all these confusing thoughts and feelings. But some of the confusion, I was disturbed to find, was going on much lower down in my body. Not so long ago, I was certain that I was going to marry Tom, that he was the only man I'd ever want. But now I found myself fielding some distinctly nonmonogamous desires.

"In some ways," I told Alex, "I was happier before any of this happened—coming to New York, getting discovered by Raquel, finding out about my father. But at the same time I can't imagine having stayed in Eagle River and never knowing any of this. That seems now like I was living someone else's life, and this is my real life."

We had reached my building and were standing on the sidewalk. Even though it was well after midnight, crowds of people still swarmed around us. Yet the only person I was really aware of was him. Should I invite him upstairs? Tati was undoubtedly out with her Mr. Billings. Alex was so nice, so understanding. And then there were those fingers, which it was taking all my restraint not to reach down and take in my hands, bring to my lips. Tom was so far away—and not getting any closer.

Alex put his hand out to pat my shoulder sympathetically and I leaned into him, resting my head on his shoulder, broader and stronger-feeling than I had guessed. It felt so good there; his chest felt so solid against mine. I pulled away a little bit and then, looking at the swell of his lips, leaned in to give him a kiss, a test kiss, just a little one.

But he reared back before I was able to connect.

"It's late," he said quickly, nervously. "What a night. Woooo!"

I was confused. Here I thought I was the one who was resisting his advances. And suddenly he seemed to be resisting mine.

Then I remembered what Desi said, about him being gay. Maybe she was right. Either that or I'd done something tonight without knowing it that had really turned him off.

But he seemed to like me—I mean *like* me like me—as much as he ever had before. In fact, he seemed to like me more, giving me a warm hug good night, kissing me on the cheek, telling me to keep in touch, to let him know how I was doing.

Gay it must be. One part of me was relieved, as I passed the doorman by myself and headed up to the apartment, that even if he was a thousand miles away, I had still stayed true to Tom. But another part of me was more disappointed than I had ever guessed I could be. It seemed as if every single one of my beliefs was being turned completely inside out, and here was another one. Just last week, I would have named Alex Pradels as the last man on earth I'd want to kiss. And now here it was a few days later, and he'd moved all the way up to number one.

seven

*I*t *was nearly a* week before I had a chance to go to the library and research my so-called real father, this Jean-Pierre Renaud character. I was too busy working, going to a handful of go-sees, but more often simply getting booked for jobs.

"They want to grab you," Raquel explained. "You're hot hot hot!"

Very quickly, I learned some of the Cardinal Rules of Modeling:

1. Be on time, even if you know you're going to spend at least the first hour of the shoot sitting around waiting.

2. While you're waiting, do not, repeat do not, eat Krispy Kremes from the catering table even though you know for a fact you could eat six Krispy Kremes a day and not gain weight.

3. Don't wear white cotton panties, or they'll make you strip down to nothing at all.

4. Don't take those hands all over your body personally: They think you're made of plastic.

5. The makeup person is usually a phony.

6. The stylist usually believes that things are what they look like they are.

7. The music blasting from the speakers will never be the music you love most.

8. The photographer sees things nobody else sees.

9. You're the most important person in the room until the shoot's over. Then you go back to being a genetically gifted but otherwise uninteresting teenager from nowheresville.

Actually I liked the part where I went back to being the teenager. Thanks to Tati, I went out clubbing a couple of times, though I refused to return to Bar 13 and, once she heard about my experience there, so did Tati. Her boyfriend, whom she always called Mr. Billings, seemed like a very nice guy—kind of a rich, urban version of Tom— though Tati was constantly agonizing over whether he really cared about her. As far as I could see, he was crazy about her, putting up with her drinking and smoking and wild ways but at the same time being a total gentleman. She'd dance away from him, draping herself over some sleazy guy just to make him jealous, but instead of getting mad he'd talk to me about how cute he thought she was, how exciting, how awful her life had been in Ukraine and how much he wanted to take care of her. And he'd ask me about myself too, acting genuinely interested in my modeling stories and listening to me agonize about Tom. Just be patient with Tom, he always advised me, casting a wistful glance toward Tati. He was sure that even if Tom couldn't always be the person I wanted him to be, Tom really loved me and everything would work out in the end. If Tati gave up teasing him and decided to go home with him, he always sent his car back to wait to bring me home—which more and more often was much later than my ten o'clock curfew. I always wanted to dance just a little bit longer these days, the nights at the clubs my only physical outlet now that I wasn't getting any sex.

The morning of my day off, I had been planning to air out and clean the apartment and then head to the library, but when I woke up I was stunned to find Tati snoring in the bed beside me. When had she come home? She'd been out with Mr. Billings the night before and usually that meant she either stayed over at his place or returned very early in the morning, flipping on the television or the stereo, smoking up a storm, and polishing off another bottle of brandy, inevitably waking me in the process.

But last night she must have sneaked in and slipped into bed without a peep. I tiptoed around the place, showering and pulling one of my T-shirt dresses over my head, making myself a cup of tea and peeling an orange for breakfast.

I was about to tiptoe out to head to the library when I heard Tati in the bed, moaning.

I went in and stood at the bedroom door. She looked pale, and was lying with her arm flung across her eyes.

"Are you okay?" I asked.

She groaned. "Sick like dog."

"Oh gosh, Tati, I'm sorry. Can I get you something? Some water? An aspirin?"

"Nothing," she muttered, closing her eyes and pulling the covers up to her nose even though the sun was streaming in the window and the apartment was toasty, despite the steady hum of the air conditioner.

She must be really sick, I decided, because in the time I'd known her, one of the first things she did whenever she woke up was light a cigarette. But today she just kept lying in bed, making little moaning noises.

"I was going to go to the library," I said, "but would you like me to stay with you until you feel better?"

"No," she said. "Nothing you can do."

That alarmed me. "Should I call Raquel?"

Raquel might not be the warmest, fuzziest, most sensitive person on the planet—okay, she may have had fewer of those qualities than anyone else alive—but she was the person who was supposed to help us in an emergency.

"No!" she said loudly.

"Mr. Billings?"

Now her eyes shot open. *"No!"*

She curled into a ball and turned toward the wall. "Go away," she muttered.

I stood there for a few more minutes and finally went out

into the already hot morning. In Eagle River when it got hot, there was always a lake to jump in, but here the closest thing was an air-conditioned shop or restaurant. Walking uptown to the library, I stopped along the way at a Starbucks, a Krispy Kreme, a big Barnes & Noble, Macy's, and an enormous fabric store where everything was so beautiful I ended up buying bright pink silk and dark gray linen and iridescent blue taffeta and rich green velvet for Desi, just in case she got inspired.

When I got to the library, they directed me to the reading room, which looked like a set they would build for a movie in which something completely wonderful happened in a library. It had a carved wooden ceiling and tall arched windows, like in an old church, and murals of New York buildings marching all around the top third of the walls, and long polished wooden tables lit with low golden lamps. It made me wish I were a scholar or a writer instead of a supermodel, so I could go there every day.

The first thing I did was type "Jean-Pierre Renaud" into the computer. My own computer was still at home—I figured Mom was holding it hostage to get me to call her, but I wasn't ready to do that. My one serious email friendship, with Desi, could take place in real life now, and I was feeling strangely liberated without the Web, especially now that all the stimulation anyone could ever need was right outside my door.

Anyway, when I Googled "Jean-Pierre Renaud" and "photographer," more than five thousand references popped up. He'd had celebrity portraits in the Louvre and wildlife pictures in a French nature magazine. He'd been the still photographer for a Danish movie and shot the wedding portrait of minor Spanish royalty. While I couldn't find an address or even a website for him, I did find a picture, which hit me so hard I slumped, breathless, in my chair.

I couldn't help but think of how strangely Alex had looked at me that night, when he was describing what Jean-Pierre Renaud looked like. If I'd had a mirror right then, I would have looked strangely at *myself*. The fact was, I was nearly a carbon copy of my biological father. Same straight black hair, same stretched-out angular body, same prominent cheekbones and dark eyes and full mouth. The only thing that was like my mother was my relatively discreet nose—but then again, relative to the beak on Monsieur Renaud, Jimmy Durante's nose would be considered discreet.

He looked . . . forbidding, with his long dramatic back-swept hair and his chic white shirt and black pants, with the cigarette dangling from his fingers and the focused, commanding look of an artist on his face. But he also looked intriguing. What characteristics of this famous foreign man had found their way into *me?* How much of my love of clothes, my visual sense, my *differentness* came from him?

I felt a strong pang then for Duke, the man I'd known as my father forever, whom I'd always loved and still did. More than once I'd been on the brink of calling him, but part of what made this so hard was that our relationship had never been based on talking. Rather we'd just *be* together, sitting in a rowboat fishing, or canoeing down some fastflowing stream, or putting our feet up watching a Packers game. I felt if we could just do something like that together now, it would go a long way toward resolving all the distance between us.

Surely some of Duke had gotten into me too: my taste for fishing, for instance, and my love of nature. But as dear as

Duke was to me, the truth was that I'd always been baffled by how I could be such a chatterbox when he was so quiet, why I loved all kinds of design and art while he had (sorry, Duke) no taste at all, how I could be so intense while he was pale and round and mild.

My mom had always explained this by saying I looked like her when she was young, a claim it was difficult to refute since her weight made it hard to tell what she really looked like. I did see a resemblance to the modeling pictures she'd saved from her early years. Especially around the nose.

I thought back now to one photo in particular of Mom. I'd never thought to question it, but now when I considered it, I saw that it held a lot of clues that Mom had indeed been to New York before last month. Number one, it was from *Glamour* magazine, her one appearance in a big-time publication, and it was obvious to me now that it must have been shot in Manhattan not Milwaukee, as I had always assumed. I could see it in my mind's eye: Mom in a velvet leggings and cowl-neck knit tunic and suede booties, chin lowered, eyes sparkling, smiling into the camera. It was a fall 1987 issue, which meant, I now knew, that it had been shot in the summer of 1987. Which happened to be about nine months before I was born.

Moving as if in a dream, I approached the librarian and asked for the specific 1987 issue of *Glamour* Mom was in. Hands trembling, I carried the magazine to one of the long shiny tables and sat down, opening it slowly to page 221, the page number I'd long memorized as the one Mom's picture was on. Then I sat there gazing down at my young mother's smiling face and at the tiny photographer's credit beside the picture: Jean-Pierre Renaud.

It was like being present, in a way, at my own conception, or at least at the first twinkle in my father's eye. My mother's smile took on a new significance: It was directed at *him*. She looked so happy—happier than I'd ever seen her. She looked *in love*.

But what about him? Was he in love with her too? Or was it just an affair? He was significantly older than she was, and he had been married, she said. Maybe I had brothers and sisters—*French* ones! He'd never known about me, but would he even remember *her?*

If I hadn't been having all these thoughts and feelings in such a calm and beautiful place, I might have lost it completely, but as it was I just sat there blinking hard and breathing deeply.

And then someone tapped me on the shoulder.

I'd been so lost in my thoughts that I leaped off my seat as if I'd been given an electric shock and let out a little scream—though even a little scream in that temple of silence caused all the other patrons to turn around and glare at me.

"Oh God, I'm sorry," said the tapper, a young woman with elaborately waved hair who was dressed the way I'd expected the *Vogue* editors to be dressed—like a fashionista. But despite her high-style clothes and hair, she had a sweet face and seemed horrified that she'd scared me.

"*Sssssh,*" someone hissed.

"I'm sorry," whispered the young woman, hunching down so she was closer to me. "It's just that . . . didn't I see you in *Us Weekly?*"

I frowned, running through the jobs I'd been doing. There was *Vogue,* of course, something for *Glamour, Men's Fitness,*

InStyle, and ads for lipstick, bathing suits, and fruit punch. They all tended to run together, because the truth was, one shoot was pretty much like the next, none of them nearly as glamorous as they looked when you were on the other side of the photograph, reading the magazine. But I'd done nothing for *Us Weekly*, which as far as I knew was a celebrity gossip magazine and didn't even hire models.

"I don't think so," I whispered back.

"You're a designer, right?" the young woman said.

I shook my head. "No. You've got the wrong person."

"I'm sure it was you," she insisted. "I was just reading it. You're also a model?"

A not very educated guess. "Yes," I admitted. "But I wasn't . . ."

"Amanda. Right?"

This was getting a little creepy. "How did you know that?"

"I told you—you're in the new *Us Weekly*! Just a minute. I'll get it."

She scurried over to where she'd been sitting and came back holding the magazine, thrusting it onto the table in front of me.

There I was, all right, that first night I'd gone out with Tatiana. But Tati wasn't in the picture, just me. "Hot new supermodel Amanda," the caption read, "hits Bar 13, here wearing a dress of her own creation. Will this multitalented newcomer end up designing more of these beautiful clothes, modeling them—or both?"

"Oh God," I said, lurching to my feet. "I've got to call Desi."

"Who's Desi?" said the young woman.

"The real designer," I said. "And my friend." Though I was walking away so quickly the last part may have gotten lost.

. . .

When I got back to the apartment, Tatiana was still in bed, still not feeling well. Mr. Billings had sent his driver with a tub of chicken soup and a bottle of brandy, but Tati had touched neither. Nor had she, I was astonished to find, smoked all day. That made me feel worse for her—she must really be feeling awful—but definitely made things more pleasant in the apartment.

I'd left my cell phone home because I knew I wouldn't be able to use it in the library, so right after I checked on Tati, I dialed Desi's number, nervous about how I was going to break the news to her.

"I swear I didn't do it," I said, as soon as Desi came to the phone.

She laughed. "Do what?"

"I was in the library today looking for information about my father . . ."

"And what did you find?"

"Lots, Desi. There's this one picture of my mom that I've seen all my life that it turns out he took. I have to show it to you. But that's not why I'm calling."

"What could be more important than that? Did something happen with Alex?"

"Not with Alex," I said. "With you and me."

I drew in a deep breath and started talking, so nervous my words were tripping over each other. "There's a picture of me in *Us Weekly*. It says that I'm wearing a dress that I designed, but I'm really wearing a dress that *you* designed, except I misunderstood the question the reporter asked me. When he said, 'Whose dress are you wearing?' I thought he meant who *owned* the dress, and since you made the dress for me, I said it was *my* dress, but he thought that meant I'd designed it, when of course, *you'd* designed it . . ."

"Whoa whoa whoa whoa," said Desi. "Are you saying a dress I designed is in freaking *Us Weekly* magazine?"

"That's right."

"Oh my God. That is so freaking fabulous. Millions of people are seeing my design!"

I wasn't sure whether her excitement was making this easier or more difficult.

"Desi, I'm not sure you understand. The magazine doesn't say the dress is *your* design. It says it's *my* design."

There was a long silence.

"*Us Weekly* says Amanda designed the dress?" she asked.

"That's right."

"And it says Desi . . ."

"It doesn't say anything about Desi."

A long silence. And then: "Oh."

I heard her blow a frustrated burst of air through her lips.

"So my dress is famous," she said, "but you're getting credit for it."

"I'm so sorry! I didn't mean it!"

"It's just that you've got everything, Amanda. You're beautiful, you've got this amazing career, you even have somebody to love. And all I have is my design talent. And now you've even got that."

"No, I *don't* have that," I said firmly. "I swear, Desi, I'm going to set this straight and make sure you get the credit you deserve. *And* the money."

"How are you going to do that?"

I had no idea. But I knew Desi was my best friend in New York, and I couldn't afford to lose her.

"Trust me," I said, though I wasn't sure I trusted myself. "I'll figure out something."

eight

*R*aquel called me in the middle of a shoot. The makeup artist answered my cell and said Raquel insisted that she interrupt me, which was breaking one of the agency's own rules.

My heart was already pounding as I reached for the phone. Had something happened to my mother? Or maybe Tatiana had suffered a relapse. At least she'd started getting out of bed in the morning and going to work. But she looked pale and thinner than ever. And she was so tired she was usually asleep by the time I got home at night, which somehow worried me more than when she was never there.

But it wasn't bad news Raquel couldn't wait to deliver.

"Jonathan Rush wants to meet you," she said, her voice vibrating with excitement.

"Who?"

"Jonathan Rush," she said impatiently. "You know, of the store Rush. It's only the coolest store in the meatpacking district. And he's one of the most influential impresarios in the fashion business."

"Oh," I said. I'd heard the name, but I'd been a little vague about what Rush was exactly. A hair salon? A nightclub? A crack den?

"This is huge, Amanda—the golden claw. If Jonathan Rush signs you, we're talking megabucks from now until forever."

I knew that megabucks in the modeling world came from being the official face (or body) of a brand, like Daria was for Chanel. Was that, I asked Raquel, what Jonathan Rush wanted from me?

"No no no no," she said, as if I should have guessed what this was about. "He's interested in your clothes! That little dress you designed that you were wearing in *Us Weekly*!"

I felt my stomach, which had been somewhere up around my heart, thud to the floor. "Oh no," I said. "I didn't really design that dress. The magazine made a mistake."

"Whatever," Raquel said. "He wants to meet with you. This is an amazing opportunity, Amanda."

"But I'm not a designer," I said. "My friend Desi is the one who designed and made that dress."

"Oh, I'm sure they're not expecting you to actually *design* a line," Raquel said. "Jonathan and his team just want to meet you, get a look at your style. They asked that you bring more of your clothes along, so they could get a feel for your gestalt."

"My what?"

"Thursday at ten," Raquel sang. "Ta-ta!"

. . .

"You've got to go with me," I told Desi.

I was sitting cross-legged on her bed, pleading with her to accompany me to the meeting, as she shook out one item of clothing she'd designed after another, trying to decide whether to include it in the bag she was packing for me to take to Rush.

She looked hard at a pink-and-black-printed silk shirt before giving it a shake and folding it carefully into the scarred blue duffel.

"I told you, I'm not going," she said finally.

"But, Desi, you have to be there. These are your clothes, your designs. You're the one who can talk about them. It's *you* they're really interested in, *your* gestalt."

"My what?" said Desi, finally looking at me.

"I think it means your style," I said. "Whatever. The point is that it's you they're really interested in, not me."

"I doubt that," Desi said.

"Oh, come on," I said, anxious to push that idea away. "This isn't some stupid nightclub or silly magazine. This is a fashion retailer that knows the difference between a model and the clothes she wears. They're going to be so impressed by you."

Desi hesitated, in the way that customers sometimes did

in the pie shop when they were torn between sour cherry and lemon meringue. You had to say just the right thing, Mom taught me, or they might walk out of the store with nothing at all. One of her favorite comebacks: Maybe you should buy *both* of them! But what was the equivalent here?

"I know," I said. "Maybe I should stay out of the way, and you should go to the meeting on your own!"

Desi's face slammed shut. "I can't do it," she said. "I'm too scared."

One pie sale, lost.

"You don't have to go alone," I tried to backtrack. "I'll be right there with you."

"No, you do it for me," said Desi, zipping the bag closed. "I trust you."

Twelve Reasons You Can Trust Your Best Friend

1. When you told her that juicy bit of gossip with the warning not to tell anyone, she didn't, not even her mother.
2. When you spend time with her, you usually leave feeling a little bit better, not a little bit worse.
3. She gives you good advice, even if you don't always want to hear it.
4. She has several other friendships that have lasted for years and years.
5. She never lies to you, not even when you ask her whether those pants make you look fat . . . and they do.
6. No excuses. When she doesn't feel like going out, she just says so.
7. If you've been friends for less than six months, she's never gotten mad at you.
8. If you've been friends for longer than six months, she *has*.

9. That time your boyfriend spent the entire day with her shopping for your birthday present, you didn't worry for even one second.

10. In any problem you talk to her about—you versus your boss, you versus your man—she's always on your side, even if that means telling you you're wrong.

11. She found you exactly the thing you wanted, the thing you didn't even *know* you wanted, for Christmas.

12. She never ever says, "Trust me."

. . .

Standing in the sleek reception area of the corporate head-quarters upstairs from the store Rush, I sucked the air deep into the trembling pit of my stomach, trying to psych myself to live up to Desi's trust in me. Modeling was easy: All I had to do was stand there and think about kissing Tom, or about gazing down on the city that night at Per Se with Alex and Desi. But presenting Desi's clothes, selling them, even merely *talking* to these important people—that felt so hard my knees threatened to buckle beneath me.

"Amanda!"

I'd gone back to the library to Google "Jonathan Rush," and now here he was before me, with his tawny skin and his bionic cheekbones, his long dreadlocked hair and his steel glasses. The son of a famous soul singer and a soft drink heir, he'd turned his own modeling career and a family fortune into a fashion empire.

Now he was coming toward me with his arms spread, as if I were his long-lost sister.

"How wonderful to finally see you," he said, embracing me and kissing me on both cheeks.

He introduced me to his colleagues, Adriana, a knife-thin young woman wearing torn jeans and a wifebeater so thin her nipples nearly poked through, and Garth, pasty skinned and bleached haired, with cold hands and a sneering mouth.

"Come, come!" said Jonathan. "We can't wait to see what you have to show us."

The three fashion titans led me into their inner show-room, all gleaming white in contrast to the blackness of the reception area. They all sat lined up in a row on one side of the long white Plexiglas table. I hefted Desi's duffel bag onto a chair and began to unzip it.

"So," said Jonathan. "We *love* your clothes."

"Oh," I said. "Thanks. But that dress in the magazine—I didn't really design it. That was a misunderstanding."

Jonathan traded glances with his two sidekicks.

"We know," he said. "The media is just so unreliable."

I felt my shoulders relax as I was finally able to take in a deep breath. They already knew. That was one major hurdle already cleared.

"It was my friend Desi who designed that dress," I explained. "We're both so excited that you liked it. I brought several other of her pieces along."

I had started to unpack the pink and black shirt that was right on top when Rush stopped me.

"What's that you're wearing?" he asked.

I'd put on Tom's old fishing vest over Tati's skimpy denim shirt and a pair of white jeans. My intention was to make it clear to this crowd that I was no designer.

"These are just old things," I said. "My boyfriend's vest, jeans from GAP . . ."

"I love all those little feathery things on the vest," Jonathan said, turning to Adriana. "We could manufacture something like that for the line, couldn't we?"

Adriana nodded. "It would have to be done in the Far East."

Jonathan smiled at me. "Technicalities," he said. "Not the kind of thing that the style inspiration for the line has to concern herself with."

I was momentarily speechless, but then I remembered that I was here to stand up for Desi.

"The style inspiration is really my friend Desi," I said. "She designed all these wonderful pieces."

Moving quickly, before their attention could wander again, I started unpacking the clothes, laying them out on the pristine table.

"Charming," said Rush. "I love the modern shapes with the vintage fabrics. This would be the foundation of the Amanda line."

I stared at him. "But it's not the Amanda line," I said. "It's Desi's line. You've got to meet Desi. Desi McKnight. She's the designer and the one whose name should be on these clothes."

Now it was their turn to gaze at me in silence.

"We're interested in an Amanda line," Rush said finally, no longer looking quite so friendly. "It would be your label, your style, you in all the ads. We're not really interested in who would do the actual designing."

"But that's not right," I said. "I'm just a model. I can wear the clothes, but it's the designer, the creator, whose name should be on them."

"We're talking a substantial amount of money," said Rush.

"Millions over the first year alone. But it's your name that's going to sell these clothes, not your little friend's."

"Her name is Desi McKnight," I said angrily, throwing the clothes back in the duffel, "and her designs are going to be famous someday, with her *own* name on the label."

Feeling thrilled with my performance, with my bravery, I zipped the duffel closed dramatically and stood tall, shaking my head and squaring my shoulders.

"I'm afraid that's not what we're offering," said Rush, standing to gaze eye to eye with me.

"Then *we,*" I said, with emphasis, "are not interested."

. . .

"You said *what?*" screamed Desi.

"I told him they were your designs, and that your name belonged on them," I told her. "Otherwise, we weren't interested."

"Are you out of your freaking *mind?*" Desi yelled. "Of *course* I'm interested!"

"But, Desi, it was a total sham! They wanted to take your clothes, and some stupid copies of Tom's old fishing vest, and put *my* name on the label, pretending that *I'd* designed them. That's exactly what *Us Weekly* did by mistake that caused so much trouble. I couldn't do that to you on *purpose!*"

"Oh, so instead you turn down millions of dollars on my behalf. Thanks a lot, girlfriend!"

I was stunned. This was totally the opposite of how I'd expected Desi to react.

"But I—I was t-trying to p-protect you," I stuttered. "I was t-trying to k-keep them from stealing your ideas, your clothes, and sticking my name on them."

"And so instead you stole my money," Desi said. "Don't you see, Amanda? Nobody's going to pay me no million dollars to stand around and smile and shake my booty. Jonathan Rush is never going to invite me in and offer to give me my own label, just like that. I don't care whose freaking name is in the clothes. You and me, we make a deal on the side, I get a piece of the money, then I can start my own line, forget Jonathan Rush."

I understood it then, from Desi's point of view. But it still made me queasy to think of going in there and letting them put my name on a clothing line that didn't really have anything to do with me. How could I take all the credit for an accomplishment I knew wasn't mine? And if I did this, what would happen next? At some point, I'd definitely be unmasked as a fraud and it would be terrible for all of us.

"I have to think about it," I told Desi.

"Amanda . . ." she said, the edge of a threat in her voice.

I wanted to say yes, I really did. But I already felt like my life was a runaway train. Doing this was like hooking it to a bigger engine.

"I'm sorry, Desi," I said. "I just have to think."

nine

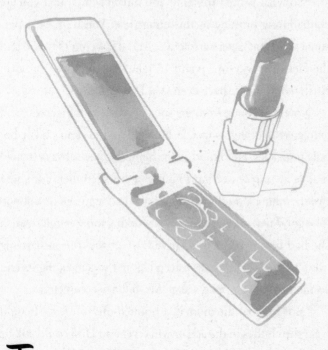

I needed advice, though no one I knew had faced a problem exactly like this. Or really anything like this.

The first person I called was Alex Pradels.

"*Mais, mignon,*" he said, which I knew from French class meant "But, cutie," "of course you must do this thing. You are no longer strictly a virgin to this fashion world of ours. You know that things are never quite what they seem to be, that we traffic in the art of illusion, no?"

I looked across the apartment to where Tati was sprawled

out on the sofa, wearing ripped shorts and a stretched-out T-shirt, watching *The Simpsons* and sucking on the ragged ends of her honey gold hair.

"That's true," I admitted.

"So what is the problem? You mustn't think that you are contributing nothing to this enterprise. You do have a personal style that is very attractive. And if it weren't for you and the fact that everyone wants to take your picture, Jonathan Rush would never have even *seen* Desi's dress."

Now Tati got up from the sofa, went to the refrigerator, and extracted an orange popsicle. She had started eating again, but only popsicles. Her mouth, even her teeth, were always stained orange or purple or Smurf blue. She brushed them for about twenty minutes on the mornings she had a go-see or a shoot. The good news was that she was working more regularly than she had been when I first arrived, when she'd been partying every night. Now she was asleep before I was most nights and seemed to have stopped seeing Mr. Billings completely.

"But I'm just the model," I pointed out to Alex. "I could wear the clothes in the ads or whatever and Desi could still be recognized as the designer."

"But your relationship with Desi is . . . how you say . . . completely symbiotic, no? It seems as if you are very close. So what does it matter, as long as you're together in this deal?"

I had no idea what he was talking about, so I thanked him and hung up. Maybe it was a French thing. Or a male thing. Or a French male thing.

What I really needed was some down-to-earth advice from someone who really knew me. I wanted, I realized, to talk to Tom.

We hadn't spoken at all since our blowup. I'd softened since then, and thought of calling him. But some part of me felt like that would be giving in, admitting it didn't matter to me that Tom had refused to visit New York, and it did matter. How much it mattered, and what that meant for the future of our relationship, I still wasn't sure. I'd been hoping he would call me first. The more time that passed without my hearing from him, the more insecure I felt, the more I wanted to reassure myself that he still cared about me, and the more nervous I felt about calling.

Wanting his advice about the deal with Desi at least gave me an excuse to call. A flimsy excuse, but that didn't stop me from grabbing it with both hands.

"Yup," he said when he answered the phone.

"Hi, Tom, it's me. Don't hang up. I need your help."

There was a beat of silence, which from anybody else, given how insecure I felt, might have made me panic. But from Tom it was . . . just Tom. "I'm listening," he said finally.

I filled him in on what had happened with Desi and the dress and the picture, with Jonathan Rush's offer and my refusal and Desi's urging me to take it. Then I asked him what he thought I should do.

"You can't do it," he said.

I held my breath. "Why not?"

There was a long silence, and then he said, "It's wrong."

"But Desi wants me to do it."

"Doesn't matter. Still wrong."

I knew this was what he'd say. I'd *called* him, I realized, because I wanted to hear him say it. But as he did I felt my heart sinking ever lower.

"I know," I moaned. "It feels wrong inside. But haven't you ever done anything you felt inside was wrong because in a larger sense you knew it was right? Or because the other person really wanted you to do it?"

There was a long silence—I mean long even for Tom. And then he said, "I told you to stay in New York."

"Oh, Tom," I said, feeling awful. "Did you really feel that was wrong?"

"Right for you, maybe," he said. "Wrong for me. Wrong for your mom."

"But Mom said she wanted me to do this."

"She didn't want you to just take off and never talk to her again."

During one of his daily runs over to Duke's bait shop, Tom had obviously bumped into my mother. I still hadn't called Mom. And I'd instructed Tom and Raquel both that they were not to give her my phone number. I wanted to be the one to choose when we'd talk.

"I'm going to call her," I told Tom. "I'm just not ready now."

"Your dad is pretty broken up too," he said.

I caught my breath. "Duke talked to you about it?"

"We've been fishing. He doesn't need to say anything. I can see how he feels."

"What about how I feel? This is pretty confusing to me, finding out the person I thought was my dad isn't."

"Duke *is* your dad," said Tom. "We're all the same people we've always been. You're the one who's different."

"It's not just me, it's everything," I said quietly.

"What's going on with you, Amanda?" he exploded. "Are you *ever* coming back? To Eagle River, I mean. *And* to me."

"Of course!" I rushed to assure him.

"When?"

That was the question. I was booked to work nearly every day. Plus, while I thought I'd be ready to go soon, I definitely wasn't yet.

"I'll be there by the weekend after Labor Day," I told him. "In time for our annual camping trip to the island. I promise."

"But for how long, Amanda? I just want to know what I'm doing here. Am I supposed to still be waiting for you?"

"Do you still want to wait for me?" I asked gently.

"You know it," he said, his voice gruff. "I love you."

I held my breath. Of course Tom had told me he loved me before. But not often. And rarely when we weren't naked.

"I love you too," I told him. "When we go to the island, we'll work it out."

I hung up the phone and, exhausted, flung myself onto the chair opposite Tati, trying to keep the lump of tears down in my throat.

"I don't know what I'm going to do," I told her.

She looked up from picking the pink polish off her big toenail and pursed her orange-stained lips. "Is it your whisky bird?" she said. "Your mountain man?"

I nodded. "Tom. I love him. But I'm afraid if I don't go back home soon, we're not going to make it."

"And that would be . . . bad thing?"

"Of course!" I cried. "I want to marry him. Or at least I wanted to marry him, before all this happened."

"And now?"

Now? I was still operating under the assumption that I was going to marry Tom . . . someday. Whether that someday was in September or three years from now or when I was thirty, I didn't know.

"All I'm sure of," I told Tati, "is that I need to see him before he gives up on me." What I didn't add was: And before I give up on him.

"Don't worry," Tati soothed. "He'll wait. I have husband in Ukraine, still waiting."

"An actual husband?" I asked, stunned. "Is that why you're not seeing Mr. Billings anymore?"

Tati drew in a sharp breath, and then to my astonishment she began sobbing. She'd always seemed so tough to me, so unemotional even when she was at her most vulnerable, curled up sick in bed. And a moment ago she was her usual, hard-as-nails self. But now she was doubled over, tears and snot covering her lovely face. I moved over and sat next to her, putting my arms around her.

"Mr. Billings don't love me," she wailed into my shoulder.

"Oh, Tati," I said. "I'm sure that's not true. I saw you two together. He was crazy about you."

"Oh, crazy, yes, crazy," she said, looking at me wildly, "but no love."

"Maybe if you talked to him," I said, thinking of how she'd pretended, that night at Bar 13, not to be interested even though I knew she was out looking for him, "told him how you really feel."

"Oh no," she said, attempting to wipe the tears off her cheeks with the back of her hand. "Mr. Billings don't care how I feel. To him, I'm just for fucking."

"I don't believe that, Tati."

She breathed in deeply, drawing back from me. I could almost see the shell hardening around her.

"I take care of Tati," she said. "I don't have nobody and I don't need nobody."

"You have me," I assured her.

But she'd gone to the kitchen to get another popsicle, as far away from me as anybody else.

Signs That It's Love

1. You *want* to meet his mother.
2. You like sleeping with him almost as much as you like, uh, sleeping with him.
3. When he burps or trips over his own shoelaces, you care about him even more.
4. You happily thumb through all his childhood photo albums, thinking how great it would be to one day have a little boy who looked just like him.
5. When you're far away from each other, life doesn't seem quite like it's really happening.

Signs That It's Sex

1. You don't want to know his last name.
2. Or his birthday.
3. Never mind listen to him talk about his problems with work or help him fix up his apartment.
4. You could describe his penis in detail but you're not quite sure about the color of his eyes.

Signs That It's Neither

1. Every time someone mentions his name, you say, "Who?"
2. As soon as you hear his voice on the phone, you start preparing your excuse to get out of whatever it is he's going to ask you to do.

3. You like the way he looks, you like the way he talks . . . but you hate the way he smells.

4. You're scared of him (even if you are having sex with him and think you're in love).

My call to Tom had raised more questions than it had answered, and I still didn't know what I was going to do about the Desi-and-Rush issue. And I was uncertain about how to help Tatiana, who was the only person on earth who seemed more confused than me. For about the hundred thousandth time since I'd stalked off into the night in Brooklyn, I longed to talk to my mom. But I also realized that what I needed was not a shoulder to cry on, but the advice of someone who both knew Tatiana and had experience with the fashion world and licensing contracts and difficult negotiations. That was Raquel.

She suggested we meet at a place in Tribeca called Circa Tabac, and when I got there, I saw why: It was one of the few restaurants I'd been to in New York that allowed smoking. Raquel was already sitting at a table by one of the long windows that opened onto the sidewalk, sipping a pink cocktail and drawing on a long cigarette.

As soon as I sat down, Raquel held out the pack to me.

"Oh, no thanks," I said.

"What?" Raquel frowned. "You're still not smoking?"

"No," I said, though I felt oddly guilty, as if she'd asked, What, you're still not washing your hair? Or: What, you're still not eating anything but popsicles?

"I thought you wouldn't be able to resist, living with Tatiana."

"Actually," I said, "Tati quit."

"What?" Raquel screeched. Now she seemed really alarmed.

"I haven't seen her drinking either. And she's going to bed early every night."

Raquel shook her head slowly, her lips slightly parted. I was gratified to see that she looked genuinely concerned, even if she was concerned about the wrong things.

"I think she split with her boyfriend. I don't know if you knew about him: Mr. Billings."

"Oh *yes,*" Raquel said, taking a gulp of her drink and lighting another cigarette. "Bobby Billings, Baby Billionaire. Do you mean they've actually broken up?"

"It seems so. But Tati is really bummed about it."

Raquel's eyes flashed. "That's good," she said. "That means he dumped her, not vice versa, so he's probably already looking again. Do you know him?"

"A little," I said.

"Would you fix me up with him?"

I was speechless, though I shouldn't have been. "I don't really know him well enough," I finally managed to say. "I don't even know his phone number or where he lives or anything like that. Besides, I don't think I could do that to Tati."

"Oh, what does she care? She's got a hundred guys dying to get in her pants, and I've got nobody but Bobby Billings."

I wondered whether I needed to point out to Raquel that she didn't exactly have Mr. Billings either. But I decided to remain on Planet Earth.

"I think she really loved him," I said. "That's one thing I wanted to talk to you about. I'm worried about Tati."

"What?" Raquel said, leaning in, her eyes intense. "Heroin?"

"Uh, no," I said, shocked.

"Crack? Crystal meth?"

"*No!* I'm not talking about drugs, Raquel. She just seems really depressed. She's not eating right . . ."

"Purging? Enemas?"

"No, Raquel! She just sucks on these popsicles day and night."

"As long as they're sugar-free," Raquel said, snapping open her menu. "Speaking of which, what should we have to eat?"

"Raquel," I said, stupefied. "I really need your help here."

"With what?"

"With Tatiana! I'm telling you she's depressed, she's not eating . . ."

"I saw the proof sheets from a shoot she did last week. She looked fabulous, better than ever."

"But those are only photographs, Raquel. I'm talking about the real live person."

"Pictures don't lie. Tatiana's moody, difficult. There's nothing any of us can do about that. Now, what are you going to order?"

Reluctantly I opened the menu and surveyed the options. I'd been eating so much food from fashion shoots—delicious, but fussy, and mostly fat and calorie conscious—that I said I'd love a burger, fries, and a Coke, nondiet. Raquel looked at me as if I'd said I'd like an order of fried boogers.

"You can't eat that. You'll blow up like a fucking balloon."

"But . . . I've eaten burgers and fries my whole life and I've never gained weight."

Raquel wagged her finger at me. "Who's your mommy?" she asked.

"Um . . . Patty?"

"Wrong!" she sang. "Now, let's try this again. Who's your mommy?"

"You are?"

"Bingo! I'm the one who knows what's best for you now."

She waved her hand in the air as if hailing a cab and the waiter scurried over to take our order. Raquel asked for another cocktail and a small salad. I went ahead and ordered the hamburger, but Raquel seemed to have forgotten her objections already and didn't even notice.

"Don't you think I'd make a fabulous mommy?" she asked, after the waiter made his escape.

"Oh," I said, realizing this question had only one possible answer, "yes."

"That's what I think. I'm *so* dying to have a baby I could steal one right out of its carriage."

She looked around, as if expecting to find a poachable baby in the Circa Tabac.

"But of course I'd want it to have my genes," she said, sighing. "With adoption or even kidnapping, you never know what you're getting. And if you went to all that trouble and then you got stuck with a baby that wasn't smart and beautiful, that would be really depressing."

"Right," I said.

"What about my mountain man?" she asked. "Have you found someone for me?"

"Not yet," I said. "I haven't been to Wisconsin."

She looked blank. "What's Wisconsin?"

It was my turn to be surprised. "It's where I'm from. Where I was supposed to look for the mountain man."

"Oh, right, right," Raquel said. "I knew it started with a *W*, but I was thinking Wyoming. Well, you ought to get busy on that. I'm ready now."

My heart rose up. "That's actually one of the things I'd like to talk to you about. I'd really like to take a little time off in early September to go home and see my family."

"Absolutely not," Raquel said.

"But . . . why not?"

"You're red-hot right now. I can't let you have time off when your career is starting to soar."

The waiter deposited our food and I took a big bite of my hamburger, which at the moment seemed like my best friend in the world. I might as well ask the hamburger for advice about my problems for all the help I was getting from Raquel.

Five Problems That Can Be Solved By a Hamburger

1. Personal hunger.
2. Crankiness.
3. Quandary over what to have for dinner (hamburger is always a good solution).
4. Boredom (if you use a lot of ketchup).
5. Loneliness (at least while the hamburger is in your mouth).

Five Problems That Can't

1. World hunger.
2. World peace (though maybe I should have said "world war").
3. Horniness.
4. Most relationship problems, except those caused by such factors as boredom and crankiness.
5. Loneliness (once your mouth is empty again).

Absently Raquel started picking the french fries off my plate and popping them in her mouth.

"Let me tell you something," she said. "There's a time for work and a time for life, and right now you're in a time for work."

"I get that," I said. "I really do. I just want to go home for a day or two, make sure everything's all right with my boyfriend, maybe spend a little time with my parents."

"Call them up," Raquel said, pulling my plate over to her side of the table. "Send them an email. At some point, things will cool off and then you can go back. Until then, I want you here."

I pulled my plate back in front of me. "What if I don't do what you tell me to do?"

She took the last fry and stuffed it in her mouth. "You signed a contract," she said. "You don't have any choice."

I picked up her cocktail and took a deep swallow. Finally I understood why I had sat through all those history classes in high school. "I'm a free human being and that means I always have a choice," I told her. "I can stand up right now and walk out of here and you'd never see me again."

"You *could*," Raquel admitted, leaning back and lighting another cigarette. "But then you'd be in breach of contract, and the agency would have to sue you for hundreds of thousands of dollars."

I flashed on an image of Tom and me, old and bent, selling worms by the roadside to pay off my lifelong debt to Awesome Models. Or worse, my mom and Duke selling the bait and pie shops to buy me out of my contract.

"Listen, Raquel," I said. "I don't want to walk out on you and the agency. I just miss my boyfriend and I have some things to straighten out with my family and I was asking for your help to try and work that out. I thought you said that you were going to take care of me now."

"And I am, I *am*," she said, reaching across the table and grasping my hand. "I don't want you to think for a *minute* that I don't have your best interests at heart. Admit it: You didn't always like everything your mom told you to do either, but you can see now it was because she only wanted the best for you, right? Like when she made you go to school and wear your boots in the rain?"

I had to admit that Raquel had a point.

"Well, that's the same with me," said Raquel. "Except my advice is more about how to succeed in the modeling world. I'm like your modeling mom."

Maybe she was right. She definitely knew more about all this stuff than I did, *or* my real mom. And who else was I going to turn to?

"There was one other thing I wanted to ask you about," I said. "It's about Jonathan Rush wanting to buy my designs, I mean my friend Desi's designs, and put my name on the label."

"Oh, you absolutely have to do that," she said, tapping a long ash into the ashtray.

"But . . ." I said, "I don't feel right about it, since I'm not really the designer."

"Let me tell you something," she said. "Who do you think designs Chanel clothes? Not Coco Chanel. She's been dead for decades. Even the designers who are alive—Ralph Lauren, Donna Karan—they may set an overall *style* for their lines, but there's somebody else, somebody invisible, who does the actual designing."

I blinked. "I know about people like Tom Ford at Gucci," I said. "But designers with their own labels like Ralph Lauren . . ."

"We can call Ralph if you don't believe me," Raquel said. "Do you want to call him right now? I have him on speed dial."

She was holding out her cell phone to me.

"Uh, no thanks."

"Okay. So, you would be like that. You would be the name, and set the overall style of the line. And your little friend would do the actual designing. And get a big piece of the money, let me add."

"We'd have to have a contract," I said.

"Absolutely," said Raquel. "We could help you with that."

"You could?"

"Of course, for the standard agency percentage. Believe me, we handle this kind of deal all the time."

She made it sound not only reasonable, but *easy*. It wasn't weird or unethical that Jonathan Rush had offered me this deal; it was *normal*. Desi wanted to do it. Why was I being so ridiculous as to stand in its way?

"Thank you, Raquel," I said, pushing away my now empty plate. Maybe she was tough, but a New York agent *had* to be tough. I *wanted* her to be tough. And I needed her to guide me through this baffling new world. "That would be great."

"Good," she said. "Now if you want, I can go into the ladies' room with you and teach you how to throw up that hamburger."

ten

*B*oth *Desi and Jonathan* Rush—along with Raquel and Awesome Models—were thrilled when I said I'd "do" the Amanda clothing line. My hands were sweating and my pen was wobbling when I signed the contract with Rush, but I felt calmer by the time I signed my separate agreement with Desi, whose entire family, cousins included, gathered for the event. I think they all had plans for her money, which I'd insisted be the entire licensing fee minus the modeling and personal appearance fees that

Raquel had carved out. At least this made me feel better about the whole thing.

Rush wanted to, well, rush the line into the stores for fall, so they'd be there when all the pictures of me finally started appearing in the magazine pages and ads I'd been shooting all summer. (All the big magazines, I'd learned, worked about four months ahead, so most of my pictures hadn't hit the stands yet.) Desi was shut away in a design studio in the building above the Rush store, working day and night like a fairy-tale princess charged with spinning straw into gold.

Barely a week into the process, the Rush people photographed me wearing the first of the samples Desi had designed and stitched up by hand, one-of-a-kind items that were whisked from my back along with Tom's fishing vest and my sock monkey slippers—sock monkeys were going to be a "motif" of the line, decreed Rush—off to the Far East to be copied and mass-produced. There was actually a clause in my contract that the original vest and slippers had to be returned to me intact or they'd have to pay me a hundred thousand dollars.

Desi was happy, at least, but frantic, with barely time to talk to me when I stopped in at the studio to visit, and no time at all to go shopping or out to eat. Alex was away on a series of shoots and I'd taken to avoiding Raquel, so mostly I hung out with Tati, who still seemed sad but was at least looking healthier, her cheeks pink and round rather than sunken and pale. Every day we'd both go off for long hours to be photographed in heavy winter clothes and furs, only to emerge from the studio into the hot, humid summer evening, the air dense and stinking of exhaust fumes and dog poop. Sweating even in our tiny tank tops, we'd bring home sushi and fruit—whatever was cold—from the shoots and that would be our dinner, which we'd eat slumped on the sofa, watching the summer crop of reality shows.

And then early on a Thursday morning of what promised to be the tenth 98-degree day in a row, I was walking through Times Square on my way to the library to do more research on my French father when I looked up and there I was, thirty feet tall and ten feet wide, wearing one of Desi's trademark vintage-fabric dresses and, on my feet, sock monkeys as big as King Kong. AMANDA, the poster read, in huge letters across the top. And then, at the bottom: THE GIRL, THE LOOK, THE RUSH.

This was it. Until now, I'd been going to all these shoots and having all these pictures taken without confronting any of these images of myself out in the real world. I'd come to feel like a real model in terms of what I did every day; the hair, the makeup, the lights, even the sliced-up chocolates had become so routine they seemed normal. But none of that had progressed to the next step, the step that didn't have anything to do with my flesh-and-blood self but was the point of everything: the actual photographs. These images of me that would go out in the world and that people—millions of people, every single person moving through Times Square— were going to see. That I was going to see myself, as well as Tom, my mother, Duke, even Jean-Pierre Renaud. Would he notice the resemblance?

I was so riveted by the unearthly image towering above me that I didn't notice how hard my heart was pounding until I realized I was feeling a little faint. And it didn't occur to me that anyone would connect the bare-faced messy-haired T-shirt-wearing me standing on the sidewalk with the enormous glossy girl on the poster until a guy hauling a messenger's bag stopped and cocked his head at me.

"Hey," he said, pointing up. "Ain't you her?"

A middle-aged woman, a tourist judging from her running shoes worn with shorts and a backpack, overheard him and glanced up at the poster and then at me.

"Look!" she said to her friend. "It's that sock monkey girl, Amanda."

The friend looked at my feet. "But she's not wearing the monkeys."

"She's not wearing lipstick either," the first woman said.

"Maybe it's not really her," said the messenger.

"It's her," said a fortyish man in an expensive-looking suit. "What are you doing tonight, baby?"

Watching *The Bachelorette* with Tatiana was the truth, but thank gosh I was sophisticated enough by now to know I couldn't say that.

"Excuse me," I said, ducking my head and attempting to walk forward. But the crowd closed around me.

"I love your clothes," a girl about my age said softly. "Are they in the store now?"

"Soon," I said, smiling at her. "My friend Desi is really the designer."

"Amanda!" someone else in the still-thickening crowd shouted. "Can I have your autograph?"

I scribbled my name on the train schedule he thrust toward me and blinked as the flash of a camera went off. The circle tightened around me and panic began to bubble up in my throat.

"Personally I think the monkeys are weird," said the tourist woman.

A wave of heat washed over me and I suddenly felt as if I couldn't breathe.

"Excuse me," I said, trying to edge through the crowd. "Excuse me, I have to go."

"You're not so pretty!" said the businessman as I brushed past him.

"Hey!" called the messenger, as I finally broke away from the crowd. "Is Amanda your real name?"

"No!" I shouted, sprinting free.

I ran. The library was behind me, but no matter; I couldn't go back through Times Square. I jogged north, toward Central Park. And every time I slowed down, I noticed people staring.

I soon figured out why. A bus trundled by, and there on the side of it was my picture, just like in *Sex and the City*. It was also on the back of a taxicab—even on the back of a horse and buggy. When I reached the edge of the park, I saw someone sitting on a park bench reading the *New York Times;* the picture, in full color, was on the back page.

"Hey, Amanda!" someone called.

"It's the monkey girl!" said another voice.

I ran, full out this time, ran like I was in a track meet for Northland Pines. When I finally saw the Central Park lake up ahead, I aimed for a clump of bushes, thinking I would rest there like I used to at Big Secret Lake, when Tom went out fishing and I sat under a tree at the shoreline, dreaming about New York and all the delights of my future. But under these bushes were two guys in a clinch, their pants around their ankles.

"Whooops," I said. "Excuse me."

"Amanda—the Rush?" said one.

I thrashed away, jogging again until I found an isolated spot under a tree within view of a playground. I could sit here out of sight of everyone, but still see the kids on the slides and the moms and nannies on the benches and know I was safe.

Never had sitting by myself seemed so pleasurable, so luxurious. Was this what it was like to be famous? *Was* I famous? Surely all the hoopla would die down. This was the first day, the photos were everywhere, people were noticing. But soon people would get used to that poster and those ads and they'd stop paying attention to me on the street.

Then I thought, with sinking heart, of all the activities Jonathan Rush had planned for me leading up to the launch of the line. More shoots for ads as Desi produced more proto-types. A press conference next week. And finally an in-store fashion show the same day that the clothes would actually be in the stores.

Cowering behind this tree to escape attention, I realized, was like a little kid hiding under the bed to keep from getting in trouble for breaking a glass. Sooner or later I'd have to come out, and when I did, the trouble would be right there waiting for me.

When I was younger, I'd always dreamed of being famous—a famous actress, singer, runner, cook, it really didn't matter. What about it had appealed to me so much, I wondered from the shelter of my tree? I guess I'd imagined meeting some star or another I'd had a crush on—Johnny Depp or Brett Favre—and I'd anticipated basking in admira-tion and attention.

But had I really wanted the attention of masses of strangers? Had I really thought that would be fun? No, I realized. In the end, there was only one person's attention and admiration I really craved. And that was my mom's.

This whole experience—not just the sudden fame, but the modeling, living in New York, meeting glamorous people— was so much less exciting than it might have been because I wasn't talking about it to her. She was the one person in my life who would love hearing every detail, who believed in me absolutely, and who would encourage me to wring every ounce of pleasure from being here and doing this.

I had my cell phone in my backpack right now. I could call her right here, from my hiding place, and tell her everything. I could imagine what she'd say, after she oohed and aahed over the idea of the poster in Times Square. Make the most of it, she'd tell me. Don't run away. Stand tall and smile and talk to people. No, not every minute of this is going to be good, but it *isn't* going to last forever. For the short time you're in the spotlight, hold your head up and let it shine on you.

Suddenly my phone rang. I was startled, as if thinking so intensely about my mother had made her call. Over in the playground, a few of the moms looked up and toward the tree to see where the ringing was coming from. I *wanted* Mom to call, I realized as I fumbled to answer the phone. Part of the reason I hadn't called her was that I was waiting for her to call me, was daring her to circumvent the strictures I'd put on Tom and Raquel and find out my phone number or just come back to New York and track me down. I was in this way too like the little kid huddling under the bed, half terrified that my mom would find me, half wishing every second that she would.

But it was not my mom on the phone; it was Raquel.

"Have you seen the Rush posters?" she crowed.

"Yes," I said, attempting to whisper.

"What's wrong? Are you at a shoot? I have this as your day off."

"It is," I whispered. And then, realizing how ridiculous the whole thing was, I stood up and said again, out loud, "It is." I brushed myself off, and stepped out into the clearing.

"I'm just walking in the park," I told Raquel.

"Well," she said, excitement creeping into her voice. "It's happened, just as I predicted it would. You're huge! A mega-star!"

"Right," I said, trying to stand tall as I imagined Mom had instructed me, but feeling the terror begin to edge back in.

"I've heard from the *Today* show and *The Tonight Show with Jay Leno*. Spielberg wants to talk to you about a movie, and the producers of *Cabaret* want to know if you're interested in playing Sally Bowles. *Vogue* wants you for a cover, and Rush is already planning an Amanda perfume. And I've heard from the agents of Jude Law, Justin Timberlake, and Leo DiCaprio, who all want to know if you'll go to dinner with their clients."

"Has my mother called?" I asked.

"What? No. But I've gotten calls from every major European designer, wanting to book you for the spring shows in Paris at the end of September."

Paris. Where Jean-Pierre Renaud, my *father*, lived. That stopped me for a moment. But thinking about him only reminded me again of my mother. "I know I told you not to give my mom my number," I said to Raquel. "But

I changed my mind. If she calls, you can tell her how to find me."

"But what should I tell all these other people?" Raquel said impatiently.

"I guess the *Today* show and the *Vogue* cover and the perfume would be cool, as long as Rush is willing to give Desi a cut of that too. But I can't act and I can't sing and dance and I don't really want to go out on a date with any of those guys."

"It wouldn't be a real date," Raquel assured me. "You'd just have to go out with them long enough to get your picture taken."

"That's even worse," I said. "What if Tom saw it?"

"Oh, Tom, Shmom. What about Paris?" asked Raquel. "You really should do Paris."

I would love to go to Paris. I would love to have a chance to wear those amazing clothes, to see the Eiffel Tower and Sacre Coeur, to order a croissant and café au lait in French, to gaze at the *Mona Lisa* and walk along the Seine. And maybe I'd even work up the nerve to go meet *him*.

But there was my promise to Tom. And my uncertainty about whether I was going to keep doing this at all.

"I have to think about it."

"Thinking never got anybody anywhere," Raquel said. "Now listen to me. Who's your mommy? Who's your mommy?"

"Not you," I said, and hung up.

Best Things About Being Famous

1. No waiting in line at bars, restaurants, the GAP, or in the drugstore to buy Tampax.

2. Adoring letters and beautiful gifts arrive unsolicited in the mail every day.

3. Everyone from strangers on the street to other famous people tell you they love you.

4. No need to show ID when cashing checks.

5. Craving hard-to-find fashion items, such as a Birkin bag or new True Religion jeans? The store miraculously happens to find them, in exactly your color and size!

Worst Things About Being Famous

1. Your late-night emergency Tampax run is reported the next day in a gossip column.

2. Psycho letters and pleas for donations arrive unsolicited in the mail every day.

3. Everyone from close friends to business contacts begin to treat you strangely.

4. Everyone thinks they already know you, the real you.

5. The only place you're really free is in your home—and even then somebody might hire one of those machines guys use to trim trees and try to take your picture through your own window.

Or at least that's what happened to me. It was the night of the day of the launch of the Amanda line at Rush. The clothes were beautiful, and Jonathan Rush even let me walk hand in hand with Desi onto the runway at the end of the show, publicly acknowledging her contribution to the line. The show itself had been an enormous success, with all the important fashion writers there to cover the event. And the sidewalk outside Rush was thronged with people waiting to get in to be the first to buy the clothes.

Everyone crowded around me and Desi after the show, asking us questions and taking our pictures—okay, my picture. Suddenly my eyes met Desi's and, without saying a word, we simultaneously started pushing our way out of the circle of press and fans, through all the people clamoring to get inside the store, breaking into a run and heading toward the river. A few photographers chased us for a minute, but they were too far back, and by the time we'd darted across the highway and reached the pathway along the docks, we were winded but alone.

"Oh my God," Desi said, struggling to catch her breath as we slowed to a walk. "That was freaking fantastic."

"It was," I said. "They loved your clothes."

"They loved *you*. Really, Amanda. I couldn't have done it without you. And Jonathan Rush, of course."

I grinned at her. It felt so great strolling along in the summer afternoon as if we were two ordinary girls out for a day of fun—the way we had been just a few months ago. I slung my arm around her shoulder.

"So are you feeling more confident now?" I asked.

"Confident? I have confidence out the wazoo," said Desi. "Check it out: I bought my ma a house."

"Desi!" I threw my arms around her and pulled her into a big hug. "There's that much money?"

"I'm still buying my shoes at Payless, but yeah. For the first time in her life, she's a landlord instead of a tenant."

I hugged her again.

And then I heard it.

The clicking.

It was far away, but my ears had become sensitized to the sound.

Grabbing Desi's arm, I yanked her down the path.

"What's going on?" she asked.

"Come on, Amanda," a man's voice called. "Hug your girlfriend again for us."

With that, I stopped short. I turned to face the photographer, who was closing in on us.

"This is Desi McKnight," I said. "She's the designer of the Amanda line. Did you write her name down?"

The man fumbled for his notebook and I spelled Desi's name for him.

"Be sure you publish that," I told him. "If you want to write about me, you've got to write about Desi."

It was later, much later, that another photographer ascended to our apartment window in the bucket of a tree-trimming crane.

After our encounter near the river, Desi and I did a little shopping, until the stares and the interruptions got to be too much. Then we bought some sushi and some champagne and some popsicles and went back to the apartment, where Tatiana joined us after her own shoot of the day. We toasted the success of the Amanda line and ate dinner. The three of us had just settled together on the sofa, where we were about to watch the final episode of *America's Next Top Model,* when Tati let out a scream and pointed at the window. I turned around to see a photographer—not the guy from the river but one I knew worked for the gossip pages of a city tabloid—lift his camera and take my picture.

Another night, I might have lowered the shades and turned off all the lights in the apartment and waited until he went away.

But that night, I was fed up. I marched over to the window and, to the photographer's astonishment, threw it open.

"What are you doing here?" I demanded.

His mouth was hanging open. He was used to people running. But he looked as if he'd never been confronted before.

"Do you want a picture?" I said. "Here, take this picture."

And with that, I pulled up my T-shirt and bared my breasts. The photographer stared but didn't shoot.

"What's wrong?" I asked him. "Isn't this enough for you? I could take off all my clothes."

"It's not that," he managed to say. "I don't want you alone. They sent me to get a shot of you and your girlfriend."

I dropped my shirt and looked behind me, to where Tati and Desi were staring from the sofa.

"Tatiana?" I asked.

"No," he said. "The short, fat one."

Without thinking, I reached out of the window and shoved him, nearly knocking his camera four stories down to the sidewalk.

"Hey, don't blame me!" he cried. He regained his footing and brushed off his T-shirt, muttering, "Dyke."

"What?"

"Dyke," he said loudly. "Lesbian. It's all over the internet. And now you and your girlfriend there are going to be in the paper tomorrow."

I slammed the window shut and yanked the cord that closed the blinds. Then I turned to face Desi and Tati.

"What's he talking about?" I asked.

They both just stared, until finally a look of recognition crossed Desi's face. "The guy by the river today," she said.

"The picture of us hugging. Somebody obviously drew some conclusions."

"Shit," I said. "That is so outrageous. I'll sue them. I'm going to call Raquel right now. I don't know what Tom will think if he ever reads something about this. Jesus, Desi, I'm sorry. I hope this doesn't make things tough for you."

"Everybody knows," she said quietly.

"That's true," I said. "Everybody knows what the gossip columns are like . . ."

"No, Amanda," Desi interrupted me. "Everybody knows that I'm gay."

That took a minute to sink in. First Alex Pradels. And now Desi, my best friend. But she was so *feminine,* with her curves and her curls and her dresses. Weren't all lesbians like Miss Koker from the printing plant, who wore tweed pants and enjoyed shooting skeet?

Now Tati spoke up. "Everybody know this about Desi, Amanda," she said.

"But how?"

Tati shrugged. "Queer eye."

But did that mean . . .

"Desi," I said. "I have to tell you, I'm not . . ."

"I'm not interested in *you,* you freaking goofball!" Desi said. "That would be like dating my sister. I told you, I'm all about work right now. Though Jonathan's sidekick, Adriana, is pretty cute."

"So what do we say to the newspapers and websites?"

"We'll tell them the truth," Desi shrugged. "It was a con-gratulations hug."

"The next week is going to be a nightmare."

A nightmare that at least would end with a flight to paradise: Tati and I were booked to shoot resort wear on a Caribbean island, an island thousands of miles from here, an island with Alex Pradels.

eleven

*T*he next week was even worse than I'd imagined. Because I still didn't have a laptop, I'd lost touch with how rabid the online fashion and gossip sites could be—not to mention how many of them were out there. While Desi and I rated only one shot on one day in the New York papers and in the big weeklies like *People* and *Star,* the sites like Gawker and Defamer did something on us every day, with multiple pictures and links to every other blog with a glancing interest in fashion, models, New York, or gayness—which meant just about every blog out there. The Go Fug Yourself girls, who'd always been my heroes, ran two items on us: one praising Desi's outfit, and another trashing mine. Even the conservative *anti*gay people got into the act—and probably got off on the pictures more than anybody.

I wanted to spend the week hiding under the bed, crawling out only to shroud myself in a burka and travel to the airport, but I had to go out to shoots, and Desi and I had promotional appearances for the Rush line. Plus, to my astonishment, both Raquel Gross and Jonathan Rush were thrilled by the publicity, summoning more and more reporters and cameras to every event, which of course attracted even *more* reporters and cameras.

The news had undoubtedly reached Eagle River by now, and I only grew more concerned about what Tom might think when I called him and kept getting his voice mail. I'd explain as much as I could before the beep sounded and cut me off. In all the craziness, Tati unplugged the phone, so I don't know whether he tried to call me back. I could only hope, when I saw him again, that he would understand and everything would be okay. *If* I saw him again.

It was such a relief to head to the airport for the *Vogue* trip to the Bahamas with Alex, Tati, Minty, and the rest of the crew. Even if it hadn't meant escape from the hounds of gossip, I'd been excited about this trip: my first venture out of the United States, first time swimming in those clear turquoise waters, first stay at a resort, first flight in a chartered jet.

Soaring above the clouds, it seemed as if we had escaped the whole sordid mess, until Alex's assistant Yuki said, "Wow, you were all over the newspapers last week."

Alex snapped his fingers. "Not another word, Yuki. This never happened."

Even I was startled. "It's okay, Alex."

"It's not okay. *Je déteste* this homophobic slander."

Alex's strong reaction seemed to confirm my theory that Alex himself was gay. Everyone in our group went quiet after that, slipping on their satin sleep masks or burying their noses in Jane Austen or the kinds of supercool magazines that fashionistas gobbled up: *Self Service, NYLON, Vice.* It wasn't until we had changed to the small plane chartered by *Vogue* and bound for our far-flung island that anyone spoke again. Then the conversation was exceedingly polite and positive, with everyone assuring me and Tati that we were going to love this place, that the food was great, the beach spectacular, the hotel total heaven.

The hotel was like one of those bungalow colonies that are perched along all the lakes in northern Wisconsin—a handful of identical cottages strung along the water with a larger central lodge—except superrich and on steroids. Each cottage had a soft white sofa and a big antique bed covered by a canopy of mosquito netting—or two beds, in the case of the cottage that Tati and I had elected to share. There was a white-tiled floor and a dark-beamed and -vaulted ceiling hung with a ceiling fan big as a jet propeller and, on the tiny front porch, two rocking chairs that looked out to sea.

We were the only guests at the place, the only ones on the entire island, except for the people who were there to wait on us. Alex quickly apprenticed one of the busboys—a young man named Winston, who was as compact and quick-moving as Yuki, to be his deputy assistant. At five o'clock the staff set out trays of piña coladas and bowls of chips and guacamole, and then we all sat down to an enormous lobster dinner. Alex had to teach me how to crack my lobster and dig the meat out. It was so delicious that all I could think about was how much Tom would love to try it.

After dinner, Tati drifted off to bed and Minty and the rest of the crew went dancing in the place's do-it-yourself disco, hooking up their iPods to speakers and singing along as they danced, eyes closed, each in their own world. Alex and I went outside into the moonlit night, cooler than New York, the air sweet and fresh as the air on Big Secret Lake.

"Well," Alex said. "Good night."

I hadn't realized we were going to bed, but just the idea of it inspired a huge yawn. "Good night," I said.

He leaned in as if to kiss my cheek, and I swayed toward him, but at the last moment I turned to face him straight on, but he was moving more quickly than I'd judged, and his lips hit mine square on.

At first we both jerked back, shocked by what had happened, and then, as if by design, we moved together again and kissed—a soft, slow, lingering kiss on the lips. But what was happening in my body was anything but soft and slow. There were zings and there were twangs, there were meltings and there were sizzlings.

"Wow," I said, when we finally broke for air.

"Amazing," he said.

"I didn't think . . ." I stopped because I was unsure how to put it.

"I know," Alex said somberly. "You didn't think you could like kissing a man."

I reared back and looked into his big soulful dark eyes.

"What the heck are you talking about?"

"You and Desi," he said, hanging his head and gesturing as if he were describing a funeral. "The things with the papers, what a nightmare, but of course I had already known about it for a long time."

"What are you *talking* about?"

"That night we went to Per Se. It was clear from then that you and Desi were involved in a romantic relationship."

"Me and . . . but that isn't true, Alex."

"What?"

"I'm not *gay*. But maybe since you are . . ."

"*What?* I certainly am not gay."

"That same night, walking home, I wanted to kiss you, then . . ."

"And so did I. But I felt you were warning me off by inviting Desi along."

"And I felt you were warning me off."

We gazed at each other for a long moment and then moved into a kiss as if our lips had magnets in them. We stood there on the beach, kissing and kissing, to the sound of the breeze ruffling the palm trees, until the tide licked at our feet. When we heard the music die down and the laughing sound of our colleagues finally emerging from the disco, we leaped behind a tree and hid there, giggling, until they all disappeared into their cottages.

"Come on," Alex said, taking my hand.

"Where are we going?"

"My cottage. I hope."

I hesitated. Tom was on my mind. As long as we'd just

been standing there kissing, I'd been able to push him away. But now that there was time to think before taking the next step, he had planted himself squarely in the middle of my brain.

"I've mentioned Tom to you," I said.

"Oh yes, the hometown boyfriend," said Alex, chuckling a little. "The beard."

"The what?"

"I assumed he was just a cover for your romance with Desi."

"No, not a cover," I assured Alex. "Real."

"But I'm here, and he's not," said Alex, reaching out and running his thumb along the edge of my lip.

"Oh, yes he is," I said. I took Alex's hand and brought it to my heart. "He's right here."

Thirteen Ways to Say No (When Your Body's Screaming Yes Yes Yes)

1. Whenever he comes near you, pop something else— a piece of pineapple, a swizzle stick—in your mouth.

2. Swim, run on the beach, jump on your bed in the middle of the night—anything to burn off that excess energy.

3. Swing side by side in a hammock, sighing at the moon. (However, I do not recommend this, as it makes the yeses just keep getting louder.)

4. Talk to him for hours about your childhoods, your schools, your homes, your friends, your favorite movies, what you want for your birthdays next year—anything and everything except how much you want to leap into bed together.

5. Talk to your roommate for hours about whether you should, why you shouldn't, how much you want to, how bad you'll feel if you do.

6. Suspect your roommate isn't listening and get annoyed with her instead of dealing with the real issue.

7. Kiss your pillow, as passionately as possible.

8. Do a lot of slow dancing, even when there's not any music.

9. Fantasize about Paris (or Philadelphia or Peoria) and what might happen if you go there.

10. Take numerous Polaroids of him that you keep under your pillow and gaze at in the middle of the night.

11. Call your friend in New York, and though she gives you good advice, question whether it applies to boys.

12. Call your boyfriend so often you're reduced to talking about what kind of bait he used when he went bass fishing yesterday.

13. Work twice as much as you're supposed to—which is only half as much as you want to.

Fortunately, or maybe not, this last one was easy because Tati did not fit in any of the clothes. Everything Minty had brought along for her to wear was too snug. We managed to do one shot on the beach together in these white flowing gowns, and she actually looked great in an overtight white tank—but that was for a beauty shot. For another shot that called for us to wear the same dress in different colors—me in magenta, Tati in turquoise—Minty's assistant laced her closed in the back, like an overstuffed Thanksgiving turkey.

When Minty confronted Tati about why she wasn't fitting

into the clothes, Tati blithely replied that the designers must have sent the wrong size samples. Minty countered that Tati had been eating far too much since we'd been at the resort, and ordered her to consume nothing but water in preparation for the next day's swimsuit shoot.

The morning of the shoot, as we were supposed to be changing into our designated swimsuits, I heard Tati in the bathroom of our cottage. At first I was afraid the sound that was coming from in there was Tati throwing up, trying to get rid of the evidence of some illicit non-water consumption. But then I realized that no, she was crying.

"Tati," I said, knocking on the door. "Tati, what's wrong?"

"I'm fat!" she wailed.

"Tati, open up!"

Finally, after much pounding and shouting through the wood, Tati opened the bathroom door. She was standing there, spilling out of the bikini she had been assigned to wear in the first shot.

Her legs, I saw now, were as long and slim as ever. Her arms were slender and firm. Even her butt and her hips were compact as a teenage boy's, even thinner than they'd been when I first met her. Her breasts were full, spilling from the cups of the bikini top, but that wasn't really the problem—or it wouldn't be when the photograph was reduced to two dimensions.

No, it was clear now that I saw her virtually undressed that Tati's problem wasn't that she was fat. Her problem was that she was pregnant.

"How many months?" I whispered.

"Six." She held up her fingers.

"What?!"

Hiding a pregnancy for three or four months—that was easy. My teachers, my mom's friends routinely didn't tell most people for that long and nobody guessed. But five months, six months—that was a different story. I thought of the few girls I'd known at Northland Pines who'd gotten knocked up and had managed to keep it a secret for as long as possible. But no one had managed to hide their rounded belly, as Tati had, for six whole months.

She shrugged. "For long time, I didn't guess. Then, I was sick. Then, I dieted."

"Tati, you shouldn't have been dieting. It's bad for the baby."

That set her off again. "I'm bad for baby," she said. "No work, no money, no daddy."

"Is Mr. Billings the father?" I asked.

She nodded, but also bared her teeth. "That nogoodnik," she said. "He don't want no baby. He just want love sex love sex—no baby."

"Is that what he said?"

"Didn't have to say. Tati knows."

"You should talk to him, Tati," I said gently.

There was a pounding on the door of our cottage.

"Girls, we're all jolly well ready for you out here," called Minty.

"Just a minute," I said. And waited until she went away.

"Tati," I said, circling her narrow wrist with my fingers. "Have you been to a doctor?"

She shook her head no.

"Tati, you have to start taking care of yourself now. Of yourself and the baby. Do you understand?"

She crumpled to the floor and started moaning. "My life is over," she said. "No more Mr. Billings. No more modeling."

I sunk into a cross-legged position beside her, patting her shoulder. "Don't be silly, Tatiana," I said. "Lots of girls have babies these days and go back to work, better than ever. And I really think you should talk to Mr. Billings. He might surprise you. At the very least, he should give you some money."

Tati put her head in her hands and moaned more loudly.

Again, a knock.

"Amanda?" Alex said tentatively. "Are you all right in there?"

"Just a minute," I called.

And then, to Tati, "You can't keep this secret anymore, you know."

She just shook her head without looking up.

"You're going to need some help, Tati. We've got to talk to Alex and Minty, because of the shoot. But I also think I should call Raquel."

"No!" Tati said, looking fiercely at me.

"Tati, I know she can be awful, but she really helped me when I was trying to figure out the Desi thing."

Alex knocked again. "Amanda?" he said. "What's going on?"

"I'm going to tell Alex," I told Tati. "I'm letting him in right now."

I pulled Alex inside and shut the door quickly behind him. He saw Tati hunched on the floor and rushed to her side, kneeling beside her. "What is it, sweetheart?" he said, rubbing her back. "What is wrong, beautiful girl?"

"I'm pregnant," Tati mumbled.

Alex looked with alarm at me. I nodded.

"Six months," I told him. "I think I need to call Raquel."

"Ohhh," Tati groaned, clutching her side.

"Tati, what is it?" I asked, moving to put my arm around her.

"Nothing," she said. "Just little thing."

But I could tell from the twisted look on her face that it was not a little thing.

"You've felt this before?"

She nodded, her face still reflecting the pain. Then suddenly she relaxed. "Better now," she said.

"Tati, I've got to call Raquel. She controls our medical insurance, our contracts—I don't even know what the provisions are for maternity leave. You've got to safeguard your health and your baby, and you've also got to do whatever is necessary to protect your career."

I was already moving to get my cell phone and dial Raquel's number. Leaving Alex to comfort Tatiana, I went outside the cottage and strode down the beach where I knew the reception was better and that nobody else could hear me.

"Raquel," I said, when she finally came to the phone after leaving me on hold for ten minutes. "We have a problem down here. Tatiana's pregnant."

"So what?" Raquel snapped. "On the rag, pregnant, you still show up for work."

"No, Raquel, she's six months pregnant. She's not fitting into any of the clothes. You have to send down a different girl to finish the shoot, get Tatiana out of here and to a doctor . . ."

"Shit," Raquel said. "She can't have a baby, especially

with Billings off the scene. I'll have to find somebody to get rid of it."

"What are you talking about?"

"An abortion, stupid!"

"Raquel, I just told you, she's six months pregnant. That's too late for an abortion, even if she wanted one, which I think she doesn't."

"Well then, she's got to go back to the Ukraine," said Raquel. "Get her on a plane back to New York and I'll meet her at the airport with the ticket."

"Raquel, are you nuts?" I said, horrified. "Tati doesn't want to go back to Ukraine. She just wants to have her baby and stay in New York and keep working."

"Did you call me *nuts?*" Raquel said. "*Nuts?* I will not be talked to like that, do you hear me? Not by a know-nothing little *farm girl* who I picked up out of the *street . . .*"

She was still ranting when I hung up on her. Then I just stood there for a minute, listening to the sounds of the wind in the palms and the birds and the surf. I turned around and saw Minty and the rest of them, clustered around the cameras and lights set up in the sand. I walked over to where they were waiting.

"We can't shoot today," I said.

"Why ever not?" asked Minty.

"Because Tati's sick."

Then I started walking through the sand toward my cottage.

"What's bloody wrong with you?" Minty called after me.

"I'm busy," I said. And kept walking.

· · ·

I already knew at that point what I was going to do, but first I had to settle down Tati and then I had to confer with Alex and then I had to walk by myself to the farthest reaches of cell phone service on the island. There was nobody around there—I could hear them in the distance getting drunk, at Alex's urging, though it was still the middle of the morning—and I sat in my bathing suit in the sand, gazing at the waves, imagining Wisconsin somewhere beyond the horizon.

As I dialed I pictured it: Mom in the pie shop getting ready for the lunchtime crowd. She was setting out single-serving pies for the workmen and shop clerks who came in for something sweet after their midday meal, plus full-size pies for the tourists and housewives doing their dinner shopping before spending one of the last warm afternoons of the season on the lake. School would be starting next week; this was the end of high season for Mom, for all the store owners in Eagle River. She'd be looking forward to shutting down a few days a week, to baking only a third as many pies as she did in the summer, to putting her feet up in the middle of the afternoon. But at the same time, she'd be sorry to see all the excitement end for another year, to be facing another very long winter ahead. A long winter without me.

The phone was ringing and I sat up straighter, butterflies in my chest.

And then there was her voice, wheezing and out of breath from (I could see it) setting down the pies she had been balancing in each hand and then rushing to the phone before the person on the other end (someone with an order for tonight, she undoubtedly figured, or Duke) hung up.

"Mom," I said, wishing in that instant that I could leap into her arms.

Instead of answering me, my mother just started sobbing. Crying into the phone.

"Oh, Mom," I said. "I'm sorry. I'm sorry that it took me so long."

"I'm sorry too," she said. "It was wrong of me to hide so much from you for so many years."

"I've missed you," I told her. "More than you could know."

"I've missed you too, sweetheart. But I understand. I really do. You have to make your life now."

"But I don't want a life without you in it."

My mom was silent for a moment, and then she said, "You had to come to that yourself, Amanda. You know how much I love you. I don't think you ever doubted that."

"No."

"So tell me," said Mom, her voice warming. "How is it? Are you having a ball?"

"Sometimes," I said. "Alex, the French photographer you met—he's turned out to be really nice."

I felt the heat gather in my face as I said this, and took a deep breath. I didn't want to go there with Mom right now. "And I've made some other good friends, and I've learned a lot. But there are some problems too."

Mom lowered her voice. "I read something," she said. "On the internet. About you and Desi."

"Oh God," I moaned. "How did you see that?"

"Google alerts," she said. "I have one set to your name."

Without my computer, I'd missed so much—though in this case, that was a good thing.

"Has Tom seen it?"

"Well, I don't know, sweetheart. Has he said anything to you?"

No, he hadn't, and even with Tom's accepting nature, I

didn't think my reported lesbianism was something he'd let slip by.

"If you don't know this already, Mom," I said, "it's not true."

"Oh, I figured that," Mom said.

"Really."

"I know, dear. You're a big star now! Goodness knows all the things they'll say about you."

I took a deep breath. "I need your help, Mom."

"What is it, dear?" she said, alarm creeping into her voice. "Just a minute."

I heard the phone thunk onto the shop's counter, and then heard Mom's heavy steps cross the creaky wooden floor of the shop, heard the squeak of the door opening, and then listened as she told a customer that no, she wasn't open yet. Then she returned to me.

"What do you need?" she said.

"It's not me who's in trouble, Mom. It's my friend, Tati, Tatiana. She's another model."

"Oh, I know who Tatiana is," Mom said. "The Ukrainian girl."

Mom had always read the fashion magazines as avidly as I did, and followed the top models the way Duke followed the Packers.

"That's right. She's been my roommate since I got to New York. Well, anyway, Mom—she's pregnant."

Mom took an audible breath. "And she's unhappy about this?"

"She's confused. She's been keeping it a secret. The father doesn't know—they broke up a while ago—and she just told me mainly because she couldn't hide it anymore. She's six months along."

"Her family . . ." Mom said.

"Back in Ukraine, and out of contact as far as I can tell. Raquel wants to send her back there, but I'm afraid Tati will do something crazy first—run away somewhere, or even hurt herself."

"But surely she has plenty of money to take care of herself."

"That's the thing—Raquel controls all the money. She can withhold Tati's earnings long enough to make things very uncomfortable. And she's also in charge of Tati's working papers."

"Oh my," Mom said. "I really feel for that poor girl."

"I knew you would," I said in a rush. "That's why I was thinking—Mom, could I bring her to Eagle River?"

"You want to bring Tatiana here?"

"It makes sense. She can't work right now anyway, and if we go back to New York, I'm afraid Raquel will force her to go back to Ukraine. I was hoping you could take care of her, get her to a doctor, help her stay healthy till the baby comes. And I just want to come home."

"Of course, Amanda. Of course I'll take care of Tatiana. I know just how she must be feeling. But you . . . you don't have to come here with her if you don't want to. I'll understand."

"No, Mom, I want to. I want to see you, and Duke, and Tom. I need to step back from this whole crazy world and decide what I'm going to do next."

"We're all here waiting," said my mom, "with open arms."

· · ·

Alex orchestrated the rest of the day like a genius. After I talked to Tati about my plan, to which she eagerly agreed, Alex instructed her to stay in the cottage, theoretically sick in bed, but actually packing up everything for both of us. Then he told the already sloshed Minty that, given Tati's illness, they would spend the afternoon shooting cover tries—magazine lingo for photos that might end up on the cover—with me. A good cover shot, Alex reasoned, would placate both the magazine and the agency after Tati and I disappeared.

Minty had downed too many piña coladas to notice when Alex's assistant/busboy, Winston, slipped away to arrange things with the charter pilot—who also happened to be his cousin and a groundskeeper at the hotel—to fly us off the island that evening. While the entire crew assembled for a festive evening, arranged by Alex, of fresh-caught fish and frostier-than-ever drinks, Tati and I followed Winston through the palms to where the plane waited around the curve of the beach.

To my surprise, Alex was there waiting for us. I was worried that he wasn't keeping the crew from becoming suspicious, especially since I had disappeared along with Tati, but he only grinned.

"Winston managed to procure some additives for this evening's piña coladas," he said. "Believe me, they won't think about where you are until morning."

"Thank you, Winston," I said. "For everything."

"You'll be seeing Winston in New York," Alex said, putting his arm around Winston's shoulder. "He's agreed to work for me permanently. Or maybe I won't see you again until Paris?"

Paris. In the crisis of figuring out what to do about Tati, that quandary had blessedly flown from my head. And now that it was back, the answer seemed no more clear.

"I don't know," I told Alex. "I don't know what I'm going to do."

"I understand," he said.

But then, as the plane's propellers started spinning, as Winston lifted our suitcases into the hatch and then helped Tati onto the plane, Alex leaned in close to me.

"Come," he whispered.

Then we kissed. Winston was watching. Tati, inside the plane, was watching. Everyone—even my mother, even Tom—could have been watching, for all I cared. I had to kiss him, as long and as sweetly as I could. Because it seemed entirely possible that this would be the very last time.

twelve

The minute we stepped off the plane in Wisconsin, Tati breathed in deeply and sighed, "It *is* like Ukraine. Even *smells* like Ukraine."

I pointed out that we were still on the tarmac of the Rhinelander airport, which in the late summer sun fairly reeked of fuel and exhaust and melting blacktop.

"It'll smell a lot better when we get to Eagle River, with all the woods and the lakes," I said. "I promise."

Tati looked at me as if I were crazy. "Better than *this*?" she asked, amazed.

Right inside the door of the terminal, Mom and Tom were waiting, with Duke hanging shyly in the background. Mom rushed forward to enfold me in her arms. Fat might not be chic, but it definitely made for the best hugs. It felt so great that at first I felt like I never wanted Mom to let me go, though then I grew afraid that she never *would* let me go.

Finally, though, she stepped aside—moving, I was happy to see, to welcome Tati—and Tom came forward. He was shy at first, approaching me as if to ask me to dance for the very first time. But then, suddenly he swooped in and lifted me clear off the ground, swinging me around as if I were a little tiny girl. Now *that* was sexy, especially when you were used to, as I was, being the tallest person in any room. But Tom was taller, his shoulders broader, his arms strong as the limbs of a full-grown maple.

I'd gotten unused to the feel of Tom in the months we'd been apart, and the unfamiliarity of his feel was heightened by his difference from Alex, who was sleek where Tom was muscled, compact while Tom was large. The contrast between them reminded me of Alex and all that had happened between us, and made me feel as guilty as I was excited to see Tom. I was unable, then, to surrender to him completely, and felt myself pull back from his grasp.

"Tom," I said, feeling shy. "Meet my friend, Tatiana."

Admitting to her pregnancy seemed to have made it blossom. In the time it had taken us to fly from our little island to Nassau to Miami to Chicago and on up to Rhinelander, Tati's stomach had popped, a perfectly round basketball protruding from her otherwise sleek body. Maybe she was relaxing too, and maybe I was noticing what I'd let myself overlook for so long.

"So," said Tatiana, smiling for what I think was the first time since the day of the bikini shoot, "this is your mountain man."

Tom raised his eyebrows at me.

I shrugged. "That's what they call you in New York."

While Tati reached out to squeeze Tom's biceps, I moved toward Duke, who was still standing back, not quite meeting my eye.

"Hi," I said, hesitating, "Dad."

He pulled me into a bear hug, but I sensed some tentativeness, and I was holding back a bit myself, so many questions still between us. Part of me wished everything was the way it had always been. But I couldn't pretend that everything was the same, and I couldn't let my family or Tom pretend so either.

Eleven Things that Felt New About Wisconsin

1. The flatness. When I first went to New York, I felt hemmed in by the tall buildings. Now I felt unprotected with the land stretching out to the horizon on all sides.

2. The sky. So big!

3. The people. So blond. And so big too.

4. The road names. Highway Q. State Road XX.

5. Cars. XXL.

6. Fields, fir trees, lakes. Everywhere.

7. Tom. How male he was.

8. Mom. How nurturing she was.

9. Dad/Duke. How sweet he was, behind his quietness. And how much he really, really didn't look anything like me.

10. The House O' Pies. How amazing it smelled. Tati stood

there breathing deeply, her eyes closed, not saying anything about Ukraine, until Mom walked over to her holding a warm piece of apple pie. Then Tati did something
that amazed me: She ate it. And asked for another slice.

11. Our house. How small it was, and how badly in need of
paint. Plus, how absolutely it felt like home.

Mom cooked us a huge dinner, which, despite the heat,
included bratwurst, sauerbraten, sauerkraut, warm German
potato salad, and warm noodle pudding. In a nod to the season, she also served two kinds of Jell-O salad: red with sour
cherries and green with little marshmallows. Dessert was a
pie smorgasbord, with a choice of whipped cream, ice cream,
or cheddar cheese for topping.

Tati ate more than I'd seen her eat in the entire two
months we'd lived together. Then she burped loudly, rubbed
her newly round stomach, and said she thought she'd go to
bed.

When we were alone, Mom said, "I'm sorry to have to
tell you this, Amanda, but they canceled the Amanda Day
Parade."

I hadn't known anything about such a parade, and the
very idea was completely embarrassing.

"Oh," I said, figuring the people of Eagle River had judged
it just as ridiculous as I had. "That's okay."

"In fact," said Mom. "They canceled all of Amanda Day."

"It doesn't matter, Mom," I assured her. "I would have felt
silly anyway."

But Mom still looked uncomfortable, and then I noticed
that both Tom and Duke were looking away and not saying

anything—not unusual in itself, but Tom was also blushing. And I'd never seen Tom blush.

"Why?" I said. "What is it? What was the problem?"

"It's that story about you, Amanda," said Mom, looking away too. "About you and your friend Desi."

Duke jumped up from the table and rushed to start clearing the dishes—a measure so extreme that it confirmed the subject could only be equally excruciating.

"But, Mom," I said. "Duke. *Tom.* That story isn't true!"

"Oh, we know, we know," Mom said hurriedly. "It's just that there was this *picture.*"

Oh, no. Not the picture.

"Where did you see this picture?" I asked.

"Where was it?" Mom said, thinking. "I guess the first place was *Us Weekly.* Or *People.* Or, I guess, both. And then yesterday it was on the front page of the Eagle River *News-Review.*"

"It was in the *News-Review?*" I squeaked. Everyone in Eagle River read the *News-Review,* the county's weekly paper, religiously. A news event could make the front page of the *New York Times,* the lead headline of Reuters, the top story on the nightly television news. But if it wasn't in the *News-Review,* as far as much of Eagle River was concerned, it hadn't really happened.

Mom, Tom, and Duke nodded mournfully.

"But people in Eagle River aren't *that* naïve. They know that a lot of that celebrity gossip stuff isn't true. I mean, of course Desi hugged me, after our fashion show, but that doesn't mean we're *gay.*"

Duke cleared his throat. "There was that interview with

your friend, in the magazines, explaining everything," Duke said. "The *News-Review* picked that up."

"An interview with Desi? So she said . . ."

"She explained that she was gay but that the two of you weren't a *couple,*" Mom chimed in. "But you know how people up here are. They think if there's smoke, there's fire."

Remembering how quickly a girl could get branded a slut at Northland Pines High, or how thoroughly everyone turned against the Presbyterian minister after he got divorced, I believed that was true.

"Tom," I said, laying my hand on his arm. "You told them, didn't you? You told them that you and I were still together, that all of this was a lie."

Tom swallowed and nodded. But there was something in his demeanor that made me feel he was less than convinced.

I looked hard at him. We hadn't had even a minute alone yet. I didn't really want to ask him this in front of my parents. But I had to know right now.

"You don't think it's *true,* do you?" I asked him.

He shook his head no, but almost too quickly. "I just don't like it."

I went over and sat on Tom's lap. I wanted to reassure him, even protect him from the pain of all this attention. But at the same time, I felt myself growing angry on Desi's behalf. After all, I *did* love her, even if I wasn't interested in sleeping with her.

"What if I wasn't your girlfriend?" I asked Tom. "What if it was even *true?* Are you saying you wouldn't like *me?*"

Duke snapped on the water and began washing dishes, something I'd only seen him do on Mom's birthday.

"I don't like people talking trash," Tom said, reddening.

"But why is it talking *trash* to say that someone is gay? Why is it even anybody's business what gender someone prefers in bed?"

At this, Duke shook the water off his hands and walked out of the room, my mom staring worriedly after him.

"Everybody here thinks everything is their business, you know that," Mom said, still looking after Duke. "I'm sure once they stop talking about you, they're gonna start in on Tatiana back there." She nodded her head toward the back room, where I could hear Tati snoring.

I had to laugh to myself, thinking that Tati would be more than a match for the townsfolk of Eagle River. But it was probably not so easy for Mom twenty years ago, which made me understand a little bit better why Mom pretended all along that Duke was my real father, why she hid the true details of my conception and her pregnancy. She didn't want me—didn't want any of us—to be an outcast.

"I better go after him. It's been a long day," said Mom, hurrying into the living room after Duke.

Finally Tom and I were alone. Though that wasn't an entirely comfortable feeling.

"So are you here, Amanda?" Tom said softly. "Are you here to stay?"

I sighed. Our departure from the shoot had been so frenzied that there was no chance to consider what it meant. Certainly once Raquel discovered that we'd run away, I might not *have* a career to go back to, and Paris might not even be an option anymore. But I realized that I wasn't sure, even if I had no other choice, that I would want to stay here in Eagle River.

"I don't know," I told Tom, drawing closer to him, laying my head on his substantial shoulder. "Tati's here at least until she has her baby, and I—well, I'll stay as long as I can, depending on what happens with work."

I could feel Tom holding himself stiff, holding himself back.

If Tom had been a different man, there were any number of things he might have said to me, things that would have been true. He could have said that he still loved me, he still wanted to marry me, and he hoped I felt the same way. He could have said that I had to make up my mind, that he wasn't willing to continue on in some halfway relationship. He might even have gotten angry and broken up with me, hoping to provoke some reaction from me—or just hoping to get away.

But Tom being Tom, he sat there with his fingertips resting lightly on my ribs—neither returning my embrace nor pointedly keeping his hands off—until I lifted my head from his shoulder and drew back. He kept his eyes from meeting mine until I finally got up off his lap. Then he stood and jammed his hands in his pockets, and though he remained resolutely the tough guy, still refusing to look directly at me, I could see that his eyes were glistening with tears.

· · ·

After several days of languishing in bed, rising only to chow down yet another of Mom's hearty meals and visit Dr. Greenberg, our gynecologist and the only Jew in Vilas County, Tati emerged looking round and healthy and happier than I'd ever seen her. True to my prediction, she didn't care a fig what people in Eagle River had to say about her—in fact, the pointed stares and whispered comments merely seemed to excite her.

"What? You never see baby belly?" she called, smiling, to the woman gaping at her on Wall Street, Eagle River's main thoroughfare. "That's right—sex put baby here!"

I had to admit, I could understand why the other woman was staring. Tati was, after all, wearing a white tank that stopped above her belly bulge and a white miniskirt slung way south of it, plus her tiny denim shirt as a vest. Oh, and red cowboy boots. Although she'd packed on maybe twenty pounds in less than a month, she was wearing the same tight clothes she always had. And if something was *too* tight—like the tank she had on now—she simply cut off the fabric that didn't fit. If that meant baring her entire basketball belly to the world, so be it.

"I love to be pregnant!" Tati crowed to me now. "I love not giving shit!"

I laughed. "I didn't think you ever really cared what people thought of you."

"Oh, yes, I care," Tati said solemnly. "I care what mommy in Ukraine think of me, and teacher, and husband, and of course Raquel, and you."

Tears sprang to my eyes. "You care what I think of you?"

"Of course, Amandskala! You are dear one to me, dear to take me to this wonderful place, dear to put me in care of your beautiful mommy."

"I think Mom is really getting off on having you under her wing, on helping you have your baby the way I guess she wished someone had helped her."

Tati stopped walking. "Someone did help her," she said gravely. "Duke help her, Amanda. He is very good man."

"I know it," I said, feeling a sense of shame begin to creep over me. Duke had become so awkward around me, and it seemed like nothing I did reassured him. "It's just that I was always Daddy's little girl, and it's weird now that I know he's not my daddy anymore."

"He *is* Daddy," said Tati. "Maybe not Sperm Daddy, but Heart Daddy."

"That's true," I said.

"Much more difficult job to be Heart Daddy."

"You're right."

"So," said Tati, "maybe in end you have two good daddies, French Sperm Daddy plus Duke. Just like you have two good mens, Tom plus Alex."

Tati's eyes were twinkling; in her new high spirits, she loved to tease me, especially about this.

"In this case, two is definitely one too many," I groaned.

I'd been relieved that Tom had been too busy with the end-of-summer fishing rush—clients wanting to squeeze in one more day of trolling before returning to their jobs in Milwaukee or Chicago—to spend much time with me. But we were about to head off on our camping trip to the island, where we would be completely alone. At least there I wouldn't have to worry about Alex calling and interrupting us, as he had a couple of times when Tom and I were with Tati, Mom, and Duke. I tried to stay neutral as he kept telling me how much he missed me, how much he wanted me to go to Paris.

"Just be sure you don't end up with zero," said Tati, "like me and my poor baby."

"Your baby has a daddy," I said, patting her bare stomach and feeling a subterranean kick in return. "Ouch, he's powerful! Or she."

"I have name, either way," Tati told me proudly. "If boy, Duke Patty Billings. And if girl, Patty Duke Billings."

My heart squeezed up, and not only because I knew I had to do anything to keep her from giving her poor kid that name. It was the reference to her ex, Bobby Billings, that really got to me.

"Tati," I said gently, taking her hands. "Won't you at least tell Bobby Billings that he's going to be a father, give him a chance to decide whether he wants to step up to the plate or not?"

"No way!" said Tati, squeezing my hands and shaking her head so hard that a strand of her honey hair came loose from the knot on top of her head.

"But what are you going to do after the baby's born?" I asked. "You can't just stay here in Eagle River."

Raquel had left several messages threatening to report Tati to immigration and to sue me for walking out on my contract. I was nervous about Raquel being on our trail, though I wasn't totally convinced she'd be able to find her way to Wisconsin. At the same time, Desi had called to tell me how great the Amanda line was doing at Rush, and to say that my "disappearance" had proven to be even better publicity than our so-called lesbian affair. If my modeling career crashed and burned, I reasoned, I'd still be able to count on the income from Rush.

"Why not stay here?" Tati said slyly, beginning to smile and swing my hands. "Maybe if you pick Alex, I take Tom."

"Hey, Amanda!" came a male voice from the other side of Wall Street.

I shaded my eyes with one hand and made out the stocky

figure of Brick Landesman, fullback and chief bully of Northland Pines High, grinning and waving both his arms over his head at me. From all the way across the avenue, I could see the sweat stains under the arms of his Packers T-shirt.

"Hi, Brick," I said dispiritedly.

"Is that your *girlfriend* I've been hearing so much about?" said Brick.

It took me a minute to understand, but when I did I grabbed Tati's arm and pulled her as I began to trot down the sidewalk, with Brick trying to keep pace across the street.

"Hey, are you her baby's *father,* Amanda?" he called, snickering. "I swear, just let me watch."

"Brick," I screamed, stopping so suddenly poor Tati almost lost her balance. And then I said something I'd sworn I would never say in my entire life—though that was before I realized how good it would feel.

"Fuck you!"

. . .

When Tati swung into the pie shop to see Mom, I turned the other way and ducked into Duke's bait shop. Duke was over by the big fish tank, cleaning off the fingerprints and smudge marks left by all the kids who loved to watch the big pike swim while their dads sorted through the flies and poppers.

"Hey," I said.

Duke looked up and then quickly down again.

This was the place, when I was little, where I loved hanging out. I'd rather be here than the pie shop any day, following Duke around, helping him hunt for bait, moistening the night crawlers and cleaning out the tanks where we kept the live minnows. In the pie shop, I had to be clean, to behave, but in here you couldn't really do much good unless you got dirty.

Now, I tore a paper towel off the roll, sprayed some glass cleaner onto it, and began wiping down the tank too, while behind the glass the big fish glided in prison.

"I sure want to thank you and Mom for taking Tati in," I said. "She really thinks the world of you."

"She's a good girl." Just like, I suppose, he'd always seen my mom as a good girl.

"How's the fishing been this summer?" I asked.

"Not bad. Not bad."

I shot a glance at him, but his eyes were trained on a particularly stubborn fingerprint.

"Get out much yourself?"

"A coupla times. Went out with Tom."

I sighed, imagining the two of them sitting together in the boat, not saying anything but thinking so much.

"Tom and I are going to the island this weekend," I said.

The first time I'd gone to the island with Tom, Duke had been against it, but Mom had talked him into letting me go. He liked Tom, after all, and Mom convinced him that camping was a wholesome thing for us to be doing together, even if there might be sex involved. The next year, he didn't complain. And this year, I guessed he was afraid that we *wouldn't* go. I suspected he was looking forward to having Tom as a son-in-law almost as much as he wished he could have me back as his daughter.

"That's good," he said. Now I could see a little smile at the edge of his lips, which made me feel braver.

"I know you like Tom," I said.

"Well," said Duke. "He's missed you."

I set down my cleaning supplies then, and looked at Duke until he had no choice but to look back.

"I've missed *you*," I said.

Right away, he averted his eyes. But that wasn't from insincerity; it was from a northern Wisconsin lifetime of keeping his feelings inside.

"Oh, Daddy," I said, welling up despite the inherent toughness of the place. I held out my arms and my dad hugged me as warmly as he had my whole life.

"I know you're my dad," I said. "I mean, not my real dad. No, wait, that's not right—I know you *are* my real dad."

Now tears popped into *his* eyes, a truly alarming development. In the time I'd been growing up, my dad had lost both his parents and his brother, whom he had gone fishing with every Sunday evening for his entire life, and I'd never seen him cry. I couldn't let him start on account of me.

"I love you," I said.

But if this was meant to calm him down, it had the opposite effect. He began weeping, his head down, his fingers over his eyes.

"Oh, Daddy," I said, moving to embrace him again. "I'm sorry if I've been weird. It's just that so much has changed."

"That's the thing, sweetheart," he said, looking up so that his eyes gazed directly into mine. "For me, nothing's changed."

That made me think of how he'd been with me in my earliest memories, when I'd follow behind him doing whatever he did: hunting bait in the spring, canoeing in the summer, skating in the winter.

It made me think of him sitting in the audience at every assembly, every performance when I was in elementary school, of him coaching my soccer team and driving me all the way down to Milwaukee when I was putting together my outfit for the junior prom just so I could buy a special ribbon for my hair. He'd talked my mom into letting me have my first computer; when he went out of town on a Rotary trip, he always returned with a stack of fashion magazines it embarrassed the hell out of him to buy.

What he was saying, I saw, was that knowing from the beginning exactly who he was to me had not kept him from loving me all along with the same full heart.

"Did Mom ever tell you . . ." I said. "I mean about the other . . ."

He nodded swiftly, turning his attention back to the tank.

"French fella," he said huskily. "Some kind of photographer."

"I might try to find him," I said, unsure how he would take that, but unwilling, now that we'd come this far, to hold back so central a piece of information. "I mean, if I end up going to Paris."

He bobbed his head once, definitively, in a way I knew meant he thought that was an all-right idea.

"Talked to Tom about this?" he asked, looking up at me from beneath the fringe of his eyebrows. Their dark mass, I noticed for the first time, was beginning to be wired with gray.

"Not really," I sighed. "But I guess we will, on the island."

"Yup," he said.

"I still love Tom," I burst out, "but I don't know anymore

180

what I want to do. The world seems so much bigger than it used to."

"Yup," he said.

"You and Mom," I said, "will you be mad at me if I go to Paris? I mean, if I decide to keep modeling for a while instead of settling down here right away?"

"Mad?" he said. "Nope."

"Well, will you be mad if I marry Tom and forget about modeling and New York and Paris?"

"Nope."

"I wish you would help me make up my mind!" I wailed. "I really have a problem here."

"You don't have a problem," my dad said, a grin stealing across his face. "You have a choice between two good things."

thirteen

I *sat in the front* of the canoe, paddling steadily, as Tom, unseen behind me, steered and moved us swiftly through the great expanse of Big Secret Lake. All of the summer people were gone now and we had the lake to ourselves, the ripples from our little boat the only disturbance on the stretch of calm water.

We paddled as we always did: expertly, companionably, and silently. But I wasn't as relaxed as I normally was in this situation, thinking about how strange it would be to be alone with him again. And how many difficult things we had to talk about.

At least it didn't feel weird to be together without speaking. I breathed in rhythm with our paddles and tried to will my mind to go blank, even though it did not want to. The thickly wooded island slid closer and soon I could see bottom, the lake as clear as the Caribbean had been, but so much rockier in its depths.

"Stay there," Tom said, seeming to see me as a lady for the first time. With a lurch of the canoe, he leaped overboard and swam us onto the sandy shore as I remained seated, serene and dry as Cleopatra.

"Well, thank you, sir," I said, smiling.

"You're a city slicker now," he said. "Don't want to muss you up."

"Oh, no?" I said, stepping out of the canoe onto the dark sand beach and tugging it farther onto the land. A lake as big as Secret had tides too, and we didn't want to wake up and find our canoe disappeared, even if we had no immediate plans to go anywhere. "Maybe I like getting mussed up."

"Really?" said Tom. "You mean . . ."

He bent down and dug his fingers into the wet sand. I should have seen it coming, but the next thing I knew my arm and the side of my face were spattered with grit.

"Tom!" I screamed. "I can't believe you did that!"

Even as I was yelling at him, I was scooping up a handful of sand myself, cocking my arm. Then I let go and lobbed it at him.

"All right," he said, grabbing his own sand ball. "Now it's war."

And then the two of us were just running and throwing and giggling, ducking behind rocks and trees, attacking and screaming, two eight-year-olds having a snowball fight or two middle-schoolers with a crush on each other. Which was exactly what Tom and I had been. I'd loved him in fifth grade, when we tore around the church parking lot on our bikes, playing a rough game of tag. I'd loved him in eighth grade, when a spitball or a snapped bra strap was the height of fore-play. And I loved him now—especially now that I felt the fun of all our years together spark and catch fire again.

Behind a piece of driftwood, I found a cache of wet leaves. Lifting a whole huge buggy mess of them, I hurled them directly at his head.

He stood there for a minute on the beach, dripping and crawling, and then he said, "All right, this is it for you."

"No, Tom," I squealed, turning to get away from him. "Come on, Tom."

"No, you've done it this time," he said, lunging for me.

I took off at a run and he sprinted after me. What was most exciting was that I could run as fast as I possibly could and still know that he would eventually catch me. Finally I felt the tip of his fingers graze my back, and then grab at the strap of my bikini, and then his hand was on my arm, and then his arms were around me, lifting me into the air.

"No!" I yelled, laughing. "What are you going to do?"

"This is payback," he said, holding me like a baby, his big hands tight on my shoulder and my thigh, as he started to wade into the lake. The water, the drops of it that splashed up onto me from the thrashing of his feet, were warm, but I hadn't been in yet, and I didn't feel ready.

"Don't you dare, Tom," I said, trying to sound serious.

"Oh, I dare," he said, nodding. "I absolutely dare."

And with a thrust of his arms, he threw me up and out into the lake, where I landed with an atomic splash.

He was laughing when I swam up to him and, with one swift tug, pulled down his shorts. He was not, as I suspected, wearing underwear.

"Hey," he said.

"Hey yourself."

I swam away but he came after me. I knew what I'd started now. As soon as he caught up, he grabbed hold of my bikini bottom. I pretended to try to keep swimming, but I knew he had me. Finally I just helped him take it off, looping it over my arm like a bracelet.

We faced each other, treading water, looking directly into each other's faces for the first time since I'd been home.

Home. I was home. Not only by being at my mother's house, or in Eagle River, or in Wisconsin, or even at this island, but by being with Tom too. By being in this exact place at this exact moment with this person. It seemed that all the excitement and novelty and scariness of the past few months were like so many clouds around a peak, but this was the mountain itself.

"I love you," I said to Tom.

"I love you."

I swam into his arms and we kissed. It was like a movie kiss, even more like a movie kiss than the one with Alex on the airstrip when Tati and I left. I shook my head hard in an effort to stop thinking about Alex.

Tom unsnapped my top and escalated the kissing, which

helped dispel Alex from my mind. We were touching and kissing and swimming. I felt like a mermaid, a mermaid who'd come upon a shipwrecked sailor. A very horny shipwrecked sailor. Tom was already at full mast and he looked so delirious, each time I touched him there, that I was afraid I was going to make him drown.

He took my hand and led me, so we were swimming hand in hand, toward shore, where he put his big arms around me and held me close so that I wouldn't shiver. We'd made love for the very first time on this island two years before, but then it had been at night, in our tent, inside our zipped-together sleeping bags, with the fire glowing and popping outside.

Now I knew that no one was around to see us, and also we did not have to work so hard at what we were doing, and also I wasn't afraid the way I'd been the first time. Now it was me who kissed him hard, who pulled him kneeling into the sand, who didn't even want to wait until he found a towel in the canoe and spread it out for us to lie on. I wanted to do it in the dirt, wanted to feel him pinning me down there with the grains of sand biting into my back, as penance for all the wanting I'd done for Alex.

But Tom got the towel and I lay down on that, which made me feel more guilty but also more tender toward him, my gallant playmate. We kissed—this was more kissing than we'd done in a long time—and then we began. Feeling Tom in my arms like that, the heft of him, the powerful muscles even in his back, there was no question that he was the one for me. I wanted him, only him, excited by his bigness against me, by his brute physicality against all that was not brute or even physical in me. It was like he was body and I was soul, and together we were one.

When we finished making love, we both fell asleep and woke only as the sun dipped behind the trees in the middle of the island, throwing the beach into shade. We roused ourselves and set about doing what we usually did as soon as we landed: unpacking the canoe, setting up the orange tent, laying out the sleeping bags, building a fire ring, gathering driftwood, and hanging our food in a tree, away out of reach of insects and animals.

While I got a fire going and worked on boiling water to drink and wrapping potatoes in foil to bake and setting the contraband beers that Dad had slipped us into the lake to cool, Tom caught our dinner. The food tasted amazing in the fresh air of the chill night by the heat of the fire. Tom had, as always, brought his guitar along, and after we cleaned up, he played and sang "Friend of the Devil" as I lay with my head in his lap and looked for the northern lights until it was time to crawl into the tent and go to sleep.

I woke up in the middle of the night with an urgent need to pee—I'd grown so unaccustomed to drinking beer, I really was a city slicker!—and despite all my best efforts to repress it, I finally crawled out of the tent and squatted near the edge of the woods, alert to any sounds.

By the time I was back in Tom's arms, I was wide awake, my ears still trained on the scurrying of little animal feet in the bush and the lap of the waves on the sand, the interior of the tent glowing from the light of the moon. Lying here like this reminded me of the nights in the Bahamas, when I'd lain awake thinking of Alex. And thinking of thinking of Alex made me think even more of Alex.

It was easy, here on the island, to push the possibility of

Alex aside, to believe that Tom was the only one for me and that Alex was merely a fantasy. But it had been easy too in the Bahamas to forget about Tom and feel that Alex was the one who was real.

Now, lying here, with Tom asleep so that there was room for Alex to sneak in, I felt guilty for holding them both in my heart at once. Yet I was also able for the first time to believe in both of them, to feel at once all the love and excitement they both aroused in me. They seemed equally attractive, equally wonderful, even. Yet so different. How could I ever choose between them?

Six Reasons to Pick Tom

1. Great arms.
2. Knows how to catch or shoot dinner.
3. Sex: excellent.
4. Down-to-earth.
5. Gets along with my parents.
6. Knows where I'm from.

Six Reasons to Pick Alex

1. Great accent.
2. Knows how to order wine.
3. Sex: theoretically excellent, based on quality of kisses.
4. Sophisticated.
5. Gets along with my friends.
6. Knows where I want to go.

That was as far as I got before I fell asleep.

. . .

On the fourth day of the trip, when we were supposed to leave, it grew suddenly cold, a wind blowing across the lake from the north. I noticed for the first time that many of the trees along the mainland shore were tinged with red and gold. The water was choppy and we broke camp earlier than we'd planned, happy to throw ourselves into an activity that would keep us warm and render talking impossible.

It had felt, during our days on the island, that we were postponing the big talk we both knew was inevitable. We had been having so much fun swimming and fishing and making love, hiking and sitting by the fire and snuggling inside the tent, that later always seemed to be a better time than now.

Now later would soon be here, and I found myself no more resolved than I'd been the night I lay awake debating the merits of Tom versus Alex, or the afternoon in the bait shop when I tried to get my dad to make up my mind for me.

When the canoe was loaded, we decided to eat the last of our food and burn the final pieces of the wood we'd gathered, building a bonfire by the water's edge, where we could easily douse it before we set off. Once the blaze was high, we huddled together on a folded-up sleeping bag facing the fire and the water, holding sticks threaded with hot dogs and bread over the flames.

Suddenly there was a streak of darkness and, from out of the woods, a whisky jack swooped down and landed on Tom's shoulder.

"Hey," he laughed, addressing the bird. "Where have you been?"

The bird, which looked like a blue jay except gray, and

friendly, cocked its head to the side as if to say: What kind of question is that? I've been here all along.

"I guess you're looking for food," Tom said, tearing off an end from one of the hot dog buns and holding it out to the bird, which pulled off a hunk with its beak and flew back into the trees.

"It's the cold," Tom said to me. "They're starting to stockpile food for the winter."

"I always forget this," I said, pulling Tom's fishing vest tight over my sweater, "how suddenly one day summer's over and it's suddenly fall."

"Yup," Tom said, sounding exactly like my dad.

I had a sharp memory then of what life felt like in Wisconsin at this moment of the year, when you suddenly knew for certain that you were facing cold weather that was going to last so long that next spring seemed like a faraway possibility—like China, or the Pyramids. You knew it was out there, but it seemed extremely remote that you would ever see it.

I'd always liked winter; you had to, to live with living here. But part of liking it had been accepting its inevitability. Now I knew there was another choice. Lots of other choices.

Whatever I decided to do right now about Tom, and Wisconsin, and Alex, and Paris, I now was aware of so many things I wanted to do in my lifetime.

Twenty-five Things I Want to Do Before I Die

1. Stand with one foot on either side of the equator.

2. Swim in every ocean of the world.

3. Study Arabic and Japanese.

4. See if the *Mona Lisa*'s eyes really move.

5. Meet my biological father.

6. Meet a movie star.

7. Have a baby. Someday.

8. Go to Carnivale (Alex told me about that).

9. Go to Ukraine (it's only fair, since Tati's been here).

10. Go with Desi somewhere, anywhere, outside New York.

11. Grow an orchid.

12. Ride in a Jaguar.

13. Ride on a boat around Manhattan (I'd never had time this summer).

14. Ski on a tall mountain.

15. Own a dog (Mom's allergic, so I never could).

16. Read all those books that in high school I thought would be boring.

17. Wear real diamonds in my ears—I mean in life, not on a shoot.

18. Learn to walk in high heels.

19. Let my hair go white (someday).

20. Dye it blonde, red, and purple (maybe).

21. Learn to make a piecrust as good as Mom's.

22. Ride a gondola in Venice.

23. See the ceiling of the Sistine Chapel.

24. See the pope.

25. Have sex with someone besides Tom.

That last one brought me back to the moment, where I shook my head to clear it and pulled my nearly charred hot dog from the fire, setting it in a fresh bun and taking a big bite.

"So what do you want to do?" I said to Tom, trying to keep my voice light. "I mean, now that summer's over."

Tom would have some work as a fishing guide in the fall

and winter, parties up for the last of the trout and salmon in the fall-chilled streams and even for ice fishing. But his rush of the year was now officially over.

"I don't know," he said. "I need to build a new tip-up for ice fishing. And your dad and I are already planning our hunting trip. Hoping to get a buck this year."

I waited, thinking there would surely be something else—something about me. But I could tell by the way his body settled and he bit into his hot dog that he'd finished.

"What if I go back to New York?" I said. "I was hoping with summer over, you'd come visit me."

He chewed for a long time. "I don't think so," he said at last.

"Why not?" I said. "And don't say work or money, because I know you have time off from work and I know that after the summer you've saved some money."

"Can't," he said.

"You mean you don't want to," I said, feeling angrier at him than I could remember ever feeling.

He took a deep breath. "Right," he said at last. "Don't want to."

This was big. This was not only the first time Tom had said these words to me; it was probably the first time he'd said them in his entire life.

"Is it because things are unsettled between us?" I said. "Is that why you don't want to go to New York now?"

"I don't mean I don't want to go to New York *now*," Tom said. "I don't want to go *ever*."

"Oh, come on, Tom, you *never* want to go to New York in your entire life?"

I said this last in a joking way, because I couldn't believe it could possibly be true. I knew Tom was a guy who liked fishing and hunting and trucks and being deep in the middle of an unpopulated forest, but still I thought he would be *curious*. And if not even curious about New York, at least curious about my life there.

But here's what he said: "Never. Not in my entire life."

"So you just want to stay right here."

He looked at me directly. "If I could," he said, "I'd stay right in this very spot, forever. With you right next to me."

"Oh, Tom," I said, tears filling my eyes. "We'll always have the island. Let's make a pact that no matter what else happens in our lives, we'll always come back here on the weekend after Labor Day to camp, just the two of us."

Now I was surprised to see tears in *his* eyes. "Not happening," he said huskily.

"Come on, Tom," I said, stung that he was pushing me away. "Don't be like that."

"It's not me, Amanda. I know with all the big things happening in your life, you don't have time to keep up with all the news in Eagle River, but this island's been sold to a developer. They're putting houses in here, big ones, and a helicopter landing pad. This is the last year anyone's going to be able to camp on this island."

"Oh God," I said, stunned. "That's terrible. I know how much this place means to you."

He smiled sadly. "Just to me?"

"To me too," I assured him.

But we both knew it wasn't really the same for me as it was for him. Tom's world was fixed, with this island its brightest star, while my world had expanded and was expanding still, with undiscovered stars spreading infinitely out on my horizon.

Maybe Tom and I did not have to break up, not now. I still loved him; that hadn't changed. But I had changed; even this beautiful place was changing. And unlike Tom, I wasn't ready to choose the real life that involved getting a little apartment in Eagle River, working at the pie shop while Tom fished, making love and having babies sooner rather than later, scratching everything else off my list but him. No matter what happened with my so-called modeling career, there were so many things I wanted to do with my life, things that involved going places away from Eagle River, away from Wisconsin, even away from New York and America. That involved doing things that did not involve Tom.

We finished eating and threw water on our fire, and shook the sand off the sleeping bag and stowed it in the canoe. Then we said good-bye to the island and its whisky jacks, maybe for always.

fourteen

I *might have set the* rest of my life in motion as soon as I
got back, but I arrived to find my home in a state of crisis:
Tati was in labor. It was still several weeks too early, but
her water had broken, and there was no delaying the birth
now. We could hear the wail of the approaching ambulance
even as I stood in the front hall, my pack still on my back.

"They're taking her to the hospital in Rhinelander," Mom
said, puffing as she rushed around grabbing her purse, keys, a
paperback on childbirth that she had read avidly and Tati had

ignored. "Depending on the baby's weight and condition, they may have to airlift it to a neonatal intensive care unit."

"*Shit fuck piss-eating shit scummer.*" This was Tati, doubled over on my dad's arm with another contraction.

"Breathe," Dad said, breathing deeply, his own Lamaze perfect though Tati's was nonexistent.

The ambulance screeched to a halt outside the house and three paramedics jogged up the front walk bearing the stretcher.

"I didn't have time to pack her bag," Mom said. "You'll have to do it and meet us at the hospital."

"But . . . what should I pack?"

Tati wanted to walk to the ambulance, but they insisted she lie down, and Dad stood there gripping her hand as they strapped her down.

"I don't know—whatever. Nightgowns. Something that opens down the front if they let her breast-feed. Underwear. Toothbrush. You'll have to figure it out, Amanda."

And then they were gone, leaving the air in the house still but somehow rearranged, as if a hurricane had just blown through.

I set down my pack and stood there for a moment, collecting myself. Tom and I had been silent during the journey home, and he'd dropped me off at the curb. Neither of us wanted to prolong our inability to say anything that might make everything okay again.

Finally I took a deep breath and headed into the room Tati and I had been sharing—my old room in the back of the house. I'd always had twin beds so that, as an only child, I could have plenty of sleepovers. My side of the room was neat, as it always was, but Tati's was the usual disaster, the pink flowered sheets a tangle, the contents of her suitcase strewn across the floor. And that was saying a lot: Her enormous bag was the same one she'd brought to the Bahamas, and she'd packed, it seemed, nearly everything she owned.

I found a small duffel bag in the back of the closet and set about gathering some things of Tati's to bring to the hospital, though the mountain of clothing was woefully lacking in any of the items Mom had mentioned. Underwear: Forget it. Tati didn't wear any. I'd have to stop at Wal-Mart and find her some basic cotton panties. Ditto nightgowns. Tati slept nude, covering herself for modesty's sake in our house with a vintage kimono she tied on to make her now frequent middle-of-the-night bathroom runs.

I packed the kimono, plus a few pairs of loose cotton yoga pants, and a couple of tiny tanks. Let's see, what else? She didn't even have any clothes for the baby—we'd wanted to take her shopping for a layette, but she was superstitious about doing it before the baby was born—so I'd have to pay a visit to Wal-Mart's baby department too.

Sifting through the tangle of fabric, my hand hit on something hard: a book. No, a diary. My heart started to thump as I lifted it and considered whether to look inside. Maybe it would hold a clue to what had happened with her and Bobby. My hands trembling, I opened the book—only to find pages and pages of tiny scribble in . . . Ukrainian. I threw the diary in the duffel, figuring she might want to write about having the baby.

That was it, then. Kneeling in the middle of the pile, I realized everything else—white miniskirts and sequined tops and saffron party dresses—would probably not come in handy in the hospital. I ran my hand through the tangle of fabric to make one final search for anything that might be of use, and that's when I came across it: Tati's cell phone.

I should have found it earlier, especially since it was making a faint beeping noise, though that had been muffled by all the clothing piled on top of it. Messages? I hadn't seen Tati talking on the cell phone at all since we'd arrived in Wisconsin—even, come to think of it, since we'd left New York. I opened the phone to see if it needed charging—was the charger around here somewhere?—and that's when I saw the message on the screen that said there were fifty-four new text messages.

Fifty-four messages! My heart did a somersault thinking that at least some of them must be from Raquel. Very slowly, I let myself look at the list of text messages. I breathed more easily once I saw that the first few were not from Raquel. In fact, I saw with amazement as I scrolled down the list, *none* of them were from Raquel. They were all from someone called BobBill—who very quickly I figured out was Bobby Billings.

"Darling," read the first and most recent, "R told me about baby. I'm desperate. All my love. Call!!!"

And every other message was a variation on that, starting with the casual, back in July, "C u Saturday?" through the pleading "Come on, sweetie" through the increasingly desperate and concerned "Where are you? Why won't you call? I love you. I miss you. Marry me."

Marry me. Had Tati known about this? I doubted it. She'd continued to insist that Bobby was only interested in her for sex, that he didn't love her and didn't take her seriously.

But he obviously took her most seriously. He even knew about the baby and was more determined than ever to see her, to be with her.

And what if things weren't okay with the baby? It was awfully early: The baby was sure to be tiny, to have trouble breathing. What if Tati herself had problems, physical or emotional?

I knew Tati had said over and over she didn't want to get in touch with Bobby Billings, but it seemed clear to me now that he deserved to know that Tati was in the hospital, that the baby was coming early, to be with her and to see his newborn child. If he showed up and Tati didn't want him then, she could tell him. But I suspected she'd be thrilled to have him at her side.

I'd never sent a text message before, but given that I didn't know Bobby Billings's number and it wasn't in the phone, I'd better learn fast.

"Dr BB," I typed. "T in hpital Rhinelander, Wisconsin. [I figured I'd better spell that all the way out.] Baby cming erly. Hrry. Amanda."

Then I threw the phone in the duffel and headed to the hospital to do what I could.

. . .

I was amazed, on arriving at Rhinelander hospital, to find Bobby Billings already there. He was pacing in the hospital lobby, his starched white shirt open at the neck, his gray suit pants as rumpled as his blond hair.

"How did you get here so fast?" I asked.

"I took the company chopper to the airport as soon as I got your message," he said. "I flew the jet here myself. I landed at a little airport just down the road."

"I know, but it's been only . . ." I looked at my watch. Less than three hours. Between navigating Wal-Mart and finding parking at the hospital, it had taken me longer to drive from Eagle River than he'd made it from downtown Manhattan.

"Where is she?" he asked.

"I'll take you upstairs to find her," I said. "But I have to warn you. She doesn't have any idea I got in touch with you, and she's been saying she doesn't want to see you."

I hesitated, but decided this was no moment for hedging. "She doesn't think you really take her seriously, that you really love her, or that you'd want the baby."

Bobby groaned. "That's my mother's fault," he said. "I invited Tati to the Vineyard one weekend, and my family was horrible to her. But that's not me. What can I do to reassure her?"

I smiled and patted him reassuringly. "You may have already done it."

I filled him in, on the way to the maternity ward, about all that had happened in the Bahamas, about how Mom and Dad had taken care of Tati, about how the baby was still way too early, how Tati and especially their child might be in serious danger.

When we got up to the ward, they'd already taken Tati into the delivery room. Because the baby was so early, they were going to do a C-section to minimize the stress on its underdeveloped lungs. My mom was with her.

"I have to be in there," Bobby said, looking around to find the door.

"Sorry, son," said my dad. "You'd have to be scrubbed

and gowned first, and it's too late for that. Besides, this isn't the time to spring anything new on her."

Dad had such quiet authority that Bobby accepted that. The three of us sat in the waiting room, like nervous fathers in an old sitcom, but we didn't have to wait long before a nurse emerged, eyeing us with confusion.

"I'm looking for the Tatiana Gudonov family?" she said.

"That's us," the three of us chimed, all standing up.

"Who's the father?"

"Me," said Bobby, swallowing hard and stepping forward.

The nurse consulted a paper in her hand. "Are you Duke?"

"I'm Duke," said my dad. "I'm the, uh, grandfather."

The nurse looked at me.

"I'm the aunt," I said. "And the godmother."

"Well, congratulations, all of you," she said. "It's a boy. And he's much bigger than anyone expected—over four pounds. He's breathing fine on his own, though he'll have to spend some time here at the hospital."

Bobby practically collapsed on the floor, as if he were the one who'd just given birth. Though I supposed he'd spent the past few months laboring under a torment of his own.

The nurse told us she'd let us know when the baby would be cleaned up and ready to be "viewed," and when Tati could receive visitors. Dad put his hand on Bobby's shoulder and began talking to him in a low voice. This was my chance, I figured, to duck away.

I found the pay phones in the hospital and dialed Tom, telling him what had happened. An hour later, he was there too, just as the nurse announced that Tati was ready to see us.

I was about to head in, but Dad touched my arm to hold me back. He put his fingers to his lips to signal that we should be quiet.

Mom had broken the news of Bobby's arrival to Tati. Rather than resisting or arguing, as I had feared, Tati had been so impressed that he was there that she couldn't wait to see him. She did, however, make Mom bring her a brush and a lipstick so she could fix herself up before she saw Bobby.

Through the crack of the door, I could see Tati sitting in bed, looking even more gorgeous than she usually did. In my brief experience of modeling, there were some girls you might walk right by on the street who looked amazingly more glamorous in pictures. And then there were some girls, much fewer, who were spectacular whether they were in full makeup wearing Balenciaga or snoring in the middle of the night or lying in a hospital bed directly after surgery. Tati was one of these.

Bobby walked slowly to the bed. He hesitated for a moment, and then he leaned in gingerly and kissed her on the cheek, whereupon she threw her arms around his neck and, crying out, pulled him close to her. Now they were both clinging to each other, both crying, stopping only to kiss.

"Oh my darling," Bobby said.

"My Mr. Billings," said Tati.

"I love you I love you," said Bobby.

"I love you," said Tati.

"Oh," said Bobby. "Marry me. Marry me now."

I turned away, feeling that I'd already watched and listened too long. Tom walked down the hallway with me.

"Pretty romantic," he said.

"Very."

"Maybe that'll be us someday."

I smiled at him. "Maybe. Someday."

"I know you have to go, Amanda," he said softly. "It's okay."

I put my hand on his strong arm. "And I know you have to stay."

We kissed then, there in the hospital corridor, and it was as sweet and romantic, in its own way, as what had happened between Tati and her Mr. Billings. Nearly, anyway.

. . .

It was Dad who, ironically enough, negotiated my return to Awesome Models and my trip to Paris with Raquel. All those years of haggling over worms and minnows had, it turned out, made him a great negotiator.

Not only did he get Raquel to take me back, but he convinced her that she had to *win* me back, and give me a raise to do it. And he got me a suite at the Crillon in Paris, not just for the duration of the shows, but for two weeks before, nominally for fittings, but really because he knew I would love it—and he knew it would give me time to look for Jean-Pierre Renaud.

I invited Mom to come with me, but though she was tempted, she said she needed to stay around to help Tati with the baby. Maybe in the spring, she said. Maybe you and Dad can both come then, I countered.

I wanted to ask Tom to join me, but I knew he'd say no, and then I'd just feel worse, so I decided to leave it.

Alex had come to seem more like an imaginary figure during my time in Eagle River, but I suspected once I got to France he would once again be very real. More real, even, than I'd let him be in New York or the Bahamas.

And as nervous as I was about going to Europe for the first time by myself, I felt better once I called Desi to tell her all the news.

"You're going to Paris?" she said. "I'm going to Paris!"

"What? How?"

"Jonathan Rush wants me to go," she said. "To research next season's line."

"Oh my gosh! We'll be there together!"

"I'm scared shitless," said Desi. "What if I get lost on the subway and nobody speaks English? What if I need to go to the bathroom and don't know how to ask?"

"I'll help you," I assured her, though the only thing I'd have on her was a week in Paris before she arrived and a little extra confidence. That, however, might be enough.

. . .

Everyone went with me to the airport, even Bobby and Tati and their baby, newly released from the hospital. Tati had, in the end, wanted to name him Bobby Jr., though Bobby said his real name was Robert, and the baby should really have a Ukrainian name. So he was called Boris Robert Duke Patty Billings, and got his picture on the front page of the *News-Review* for being the longest, thinnest baby ever born in Vilas County.

Bobby actually rented a beautiful old lodge on Big Secret Lake where he and Tati and the baby were staying, though they spent a lot of time with Mom. When Dad was negotiating my return to Awesome, he also worked out amnesty for Tatiana, who planned to go with Bobby and baby Boris later in the fall to New York. As soon as she secured her divorce from her Ukrainian husband, she and Bobby planned to get married in spectacular style. She was already slimmer than she'd been before she got pregnant, and ready for any catwalk.

After I checked in for my flight, Tom and I went outside to spend a little time alone together before I had to leave. Even though it was still September, fall had definitely arrived. The trees were blazing and it was so nippy I pulled my sweater tightly around my body. Tom put his arm around me to warm me up and led me across the lawn toward the little grove of trees, pebbles and twigs biting into my feet through my sock monkey slippers, which I was wearing this time for luck.

We perched together atop a rock and sat there close together, Tom's arm still tight around me.

"Will you marry me?" Tom said suddenly.

I turned to him, my mouth open in shock, afraid he'd misunderstood everything that had passed between us over the past few weeks, worried that he might not even realize where I was going today.

"I was thinking maybe 2011," he said lightly. "Early September. We could boat everybody over to the island."

I began to smile, nodding. "2011. That's a possibility. Though I might not be available until 2015."

Tom waggled his head. "I might be able to do 2015. Though I'd definitely want to firm things up between us by 2020."

"Let's see," I said. "In 2020, I'll be thirty-one. I guess that would be the upper limit of when I'd want to get married and start having babies."

"And I'll be thirty-five," said Tom. "Bobby Billings's age."

"That's a good age to have a family."

"Okay," said Tom. "Then it's settled. To seal the deal, I brought you this."

He reached into the front pocket of his green wool shirt and drew out a long gray feather.

"What is it?"

"A whisky jack feather. From the island."

"Oh, Tom."

"And this," he said, reaching into a pouch on his new fishing vest and drawing out a round black rock, about the size of a donut hole.

"What's this?"

"It's a meteorite." He grinned. "I found it in the snow when I was tracking an elk last year."

"Wow," I said, turning it over, thinking how much more special it was than anything you could buy in a store. "I was going to buy you a boat."

"Thanks, Amanda, but a guy can't let his girlfriend buy him a guide boat. Besides, I'm going to be able to buy my own. Bobby wants to invest in my business. Get some high rollers from New York out here to fish, charge them ten times what I charge now. He's talking to those developers about buying the whole island, turning the place into a high-class ecologically friendly fishing camp."

I looked hard at Tom, whose face was lit up with delight. "That's fantastic, Tom," I said. "Really."

"Yeah. Maybe one of these days I'll even make as much money as you."

Was there resentment in that statement? He continued

to look happy and innocent, but I couldn't help feeling a tad defensive. "Models are like football players," I told him. "They make a lot because their career span is limited."

Tom lifted his arm from around my shoulder and took my hand.

"I know," he said. "I may be a regular guy, but I'm trying not to be stupid."

"It's all right," I said, patting his hand.

"No," he said, sitting up taller. "It's not. Maybe I can't be the guy who goes to Paris or New York with you, Amanda, but I want to love you in other ways that matter. And right now, I know that means letting you go. Letting you go to pursue your career, and find your French father, and do . . . whatever else you want to do. And I just hope that in 2011 or 2015 or 2020 you'll want to come back here to be with me."

"I hope so too," I said. Sincerely.

We kissed then, not a big dramatic kiss but the kind of solid kiss that seals something. Our kiss was interrupted by the roar of a plane descending from the east and swooping down onto the runway just beyond where we sat. It was my plane, bound for Chicago, where I'd catch another directly for Paris.

Eight Things I Was Going to Miss

1. Tom's kisses.
2. My mom's wisdom, and her apple pie.
3. The sense of peace and plenty in the bait shop.
4. Watching little Boris grow.
5. Bratwurst, fried walleye, and hot fudge milk shakes.
6. The absolute quiet you could find within fifteen minutes of wherever you found yourself in northern Wisconsin.

7. Understanding everything everybody around you was saying, even when they weren't saying anything.

8. Feeling sure about what was going to happen next.

Eight Things I Was Looking Forward To

1. Seeing the Eiffel Tower.

2. Seeing Alex again.

3. Showing Desi the new world I'd just discovered.

4. Finding out more about my biological father. I hope.

5. Eating a croissant in a place where everyone knew how to pronounce it.

6. Staying at a fancy hotel.

7. Actually being part of the best fashion shows in the entire world (although if I let myself think about this too much, my feet started to sweat inside the sock monkey slippers).

8. Being alone on the plane with time to meditate, and nothing to look at but ocean and sky.

This time, everyone was gathered at the gate. Tom and Dad hugged and kissed me, and did not hurry off. Tati and Bobby and even the baby hugged and kissed me, three new people in my life to love. And Mom hugged me longest of all, since she was not coming with me this time. I said good-bye to everyone, and went through the gate alone.

The must-have accessories of the season...

Look for these great reads from Downtown Press!

Accidental It Girl
Libby Street
Sometimes, accidents
happen for a reason.

The Starter Wife
Gigi Levangie Grazer
Been there...married that.

Still Thinking of You
Adele Parks
... even though I shouldn't be.

Going Home
Harriet Evans
They say love feels like going
home . . . but what if your home
is no longer there?

Always & Forever
Cathy Kelly
Trouble lasts a moment.
Friendship lasts forever.

Nearlyweds
Beth Kendrick
"I nearly do...."

Real Women Eat Beef
Tracy McArdle
Sometimes a girl just needs
to be satisfied.

Available wherever books are sold or at www.downtownpress.com.

Great storytelling just got a new address.

DOWNTOWN PRESS
A Division of Simon & Schuster
A CBS COMPANY

15609

Life is always a little sweeter with a book from Downtown Press!

ENSLAVE ME SWEETLY
Gena Showalter

She has the heart of a killer…
and the body of an angel.

CARPOOL CONFIDENTIAL
Jessica Benson

You'll be amazed what you
can learn riding shotgun.

THE MAN SHE THOUGHT SHE KNEW
Shari Shattuck

What kind of secrets is
her lover keeping?
The deadly kind…

INVISIBLE LIVES
Anjali Banerjee

She can sense your heart's
desire. But what does *her*
heart desire?

LOOKING FOR MR. GOODBUNNY
Kathleen O'Reilly

Fixing other people's problems
is easy. It's fixing your own
that's hard.

SEX AND THE SOUTH BEACH CHICAS
Caridad Piñeiro

Shake things up with four
girls who know how to spice
things up…

WHY MOMS ARE WEIRD
Pamela Ribon

And you thought *your* family
was weird.